THE DAY
AFTER
THE PARTY

BOOKS BY NICOLE TROPE

My Daughter's Secret

The Boy in the Photo

The Nowhere Girl

The Life She Left Behind

The Girl Who Never Came Home

Bring Him Home

The Family Across the Street

The Mother's Fault

The Stepchild

His Other Wife

The Foster Family

The Stay-at-Home Mother

The Truth about the Accident

THE DAY AFTER THE PARTY

NICOLE TROPE

bookouture

Published by Bookouture in 2023

An imprint of Storyfire Ltd.
Carmelite House
50 Victoria Embankment
London EC4Y 0DZ

www.bookouture.com

ISBN: 978-1-83790-892-9
eBook ISBN: 978-1-83790-891-2

For D, M, I and J.

INVITATION

Please join us for Katelyn's birthday party.
There'll be lots to drink and the food will be hearty.

Everything starts on the dot of 7.
We know the babysitters leave by 11.

Winter Wonderland is the theme.
Dress in silver and white if you want to be seen.

Please let us know if you can come.
27th of May for tremendous fun.

PROLOGUE

Saturday Night, 27 May, 11.15 p.m.

A champagne bottle lies on its side on a trestle table covered in a snow-white cloth, pale-yellow liquid dribbling out onto the rug below, a dark puddle forming.

Against one wall, a silver banner hangs listlessly, pulled from the wall and half folded. Black letters, *HAPPY BIRTHDAY K* visible.

Bright lights seek out the chaos and mess in the room, scattered chip crumbs on every surface, plastic cups stacked up, tiny amounts of lurid pink-coloured liquid swimming in the bottom of each one.

Silver snowflakes that sparkled in the low light reveal themselves as cheap plastic, along with the silver tinsel that is looped around tables and along the walls. The fairy lights hanging from the ceiling no longer blink little white shiny stars.

The Winter Wonderland has disappeared, only the detritus of four hours of festivities remains.

Most of the guests have gone home. Only the broken-hearted, the hurt and the angry are left.

'Look what you've done, look at this mess,' she screams.

'Me?' he answers. 'Me?' Fury in his voice. 'What about what you've done, what about what you did?'

'I don't know what you're talking about. What are you talking about?'

'How drunk are you?' he spits.

'Look at this mess,' she repeats.

'Are you crazy?' he asks. 'Are you crazy, or just trying to drive me crazy?'

'What do you mean? Look at this mess.'

'Stop yelling at me. This is your fault.'

'What are you talking about?' she screams, frustration bringing tears. Round and around they go, confusion and despair on both sides.

In the corner, leaning against the wall with her arms folded, she waits for them to finish, waits for it to be her turn to speak, her turn to ask questions. Stepping forward, she stands the bottle of champagne upright, stares down at the mess on the rug and then moves away, letting the puddle spread and stain, a small smile on her face.

This is what I wanted, she thinks.

This is exactly what I wanted.

ONE

KATELYN

Monday, 3 a.m. – Two Days After the Party

Turning on her side because there's a slight twinge in her back, Katelyn opens her eyes and is surprised to see Toby slumped in a chair next to the bed, his eyes closed and his head tilted. He looks really uncomfortable. She doesn't recognise the chair he's sitting in. Blinking rapidly in case this is a dream, she stretches out her leg, feeling her foot move against rough sheets. She's definitely awake.

'What are you doing?' she asks him, and he lifts his head and sighs.

'I was just getting some sleep,' he says, rubbing at his brown eyes under his glasses and then running his hands through his messy brown curls. The room is dim with light coming in from outside. Unfamiliar shapes loom in corners and she can hear someone speaking and then the sound of a phone ringing somewhere.

Toby leans forward and switches on a lamp sitting on a side table next to her. She doesn't recognise the lamp, so despite feeling wide awake this must be a dream. It has the vividly real feeling of some of her dreams, the ones that leave her with a racing heart and dry mouth, the ones that she is always relieved to wake up from. But those dreams are usually ones in which she is being chased, or driving a car without brakes, or has lost sight of Harper. They don't involve her husband sitting in an unfamiliar chair next to an unfamiliar bed.

'Why don't you just get into bed?' says Katelyn, and then she takes a good look around the room, feels the scratchy sheets again and catches a strange, sharp, chemical scent of something.

This is not their bedroom and she is not in their bed.

'Where are we?' she asks and Toby sighs again, slumping forward on the chair and dropping his head into his hands. 'Read the piece of paper in your hand, Kate,' he says, the words heavy with exhaustion, and only then does she notice that she is clutching a piece of blue notebook paper, softly scrunched from her hands. She sits up in the bed she is lying in, listening to the crackle of something plastic beneath her, and takes a look at the note while Toby hangs his head.

You are in a hospital.

Harper is fine and with my mum.

You've lost your memory.

You haven't had a stroke.

You've had an MRI and ECG and everything is fine.

You have something called Transient Global Amnesia.

Your lost hours of memory have shown up on the MRI as a black dot.

*You aren't able to form new memories so you keep forgetting
things I've told you.*

Today is Sunday.

This should be temporary.

Katelyn looks at Toby and then she reads the words again.
The words *black dot* and *amnesia* jumping out at her. Toby lifts
his head and watches her read the note. Katelyn feels her lips
moving as she reads. She reaches up to her head, touching the
back of her skull, expecting to find something there, expecting
to be able to feel the black dot. She reads the words again.

'Technically, I suppose, it's Monday now so I should change
that last one,' he says, sounding defeated. Why does he sound
like that?

Katelyn reads the list one more time. 'I don't understand,'
she says. She is obviously in a hospital bed in a hospital room
and something has happened to her. Inside her, panic rises up
from her toes, shooting through her body and causing her heart
to race and her head to pound. 'I don't understand,' she says
again.

'Read the list, Kate,' says Toby, staring at the wall next to
her bed, his voice robotic as though saying this bores or irritates
him; or as though he has repeated these same words many,
many times.

'I've read the list, Toby,' she replies, shouting now, 'and I
know what it says. How long have I been here?'

'What does it say?' he asks, finally looking at her, cocking
his head to the side and examining her. 'Without looking at it
again, tell me what it says.'

'It says that I've lost my memory and that Harper is with
your mum and that it's Sunday, although you told me that, technically, it's Monday so it must be early Monday morning

because it's dark outside. I know what the list says, Toby,' she snaps, exasperated at the feeling of disorientation swirling around her. She wants to wipe her eyes to get rid of the fog in front of her but she knows that her eyes are fine.

'Let me get the doctor,' says Toby excitedly, jumping up from his chair. He is wearing his smart black jeans and the bright white shirt she bought for him for his birthday. 'It will be nice to wear to a party,' she remembers telling him when he opened it. The silver accents on the sleeves looked good against his honey-coloured skin. The shirt is rumpled, the sleeves rolled up. It looks like he's slept in his clothes.

'What's the time?' she asks, checking around her for her phone. 'Where's my phone?'

'It's 3 a.m. on Monday morning,' says Toby.

'I doubt there's going to be a doctor around now,' she says.

'So, you know where you are?' he asks excitedly.

'Toby, I'm not an idiot,' she says. 'Why are you talking to me like I am one?'

At the door to the room, Toby stops and looks back at her. 'Can you tell me what the list said, Kate, I mean without looking at it again?' And now his voice is filled with desperate hope. She has no idea what's going on but her disorientation rumbles itself into pure irritation.

Katelyn scrunches up the list and throws the ball of blue paper across the room, frustrated at being asked the same questions over and over again. She has already answered him. 'Your list, and I know you wrote it because I recognise your handwriting, says that I have lost my memory and that Harper is with your mum and if it's Monday I hope she has her backpack because it's a preschool day.' Is he making fun of her, is that what this is? Is this some kind of colossal joke?

'I'll get someone,' says Toby with a wide smile and he leaves before Katelyn can ask him anything else.

Katelyn looks around the room where white slatted blinds

are closed against the night. There is a television bolted high up on the wall and a door that must lead to a bathroom. She hopes it does because she is suddenly in desperate need of a toilet. Getting out of bed, she moves slowly, gingerly at first in case something is injured, but then more quickly as she feels her body move just the way she is used to. There is no pain anywhere. She is wearing a hospital gown and underwear that feels like it's made of paper. Where are her clothes? What was she wearing when she got here?

In the bathroom she can see that her face is clean of make-up, only a slight smudge of black under her eyes that she wipes at with her fingers. Her highlighted brown hair is a tangled mess. She runs her fingers through it as she stares at her shadowed green eyes, squinting against the bright light of the bathroom at the wrinkles she always catalogues in the morning. What exactly has happened to her? She lifts the gown and looks at her body in the mirror, turning around and searching for a bruise or a cut or something to tell her that she's had some kind of accident, but she looks exactly the same as always. 'You need to start exercising,' she tells herself, just like she does every morning.

Climbing back into the bed she sits up and looks around for the remote for the television, remembering a television series where a man wakes from a coma to discover that the whole world had been overtaken by zombies. Where is Toby and what happens if he doesn't come back? 'Don't be ridiculous,' she mutters. Harper wouldn't be with Toby's mother if the world had been overtaken by zombies. Maybe she banged her head? Reaching up, she uses both hands to forcefully examine her skull again for bruising but there's nothing, although there is a headache taking hold.

It seems possible that the entire world has changed and she hasn't been there to watch it. Everything feels terribly wrong... off. Aside from her pounding head and some nausea, she thinks she's okay. Is she?

The door opens and Toby returns with a nurse dressed in blue scrubs, her short blonde hair slicked back and a smile on her face. Katelyn takes a deep relieved breath. At least he came back. No zombies then.

'Hello, Katelyn. I'm Amanda. I've been looking after you for the past few hours.' The nurse stands next to the bed and grasps Katelyn's wrist with her fingers, glancing briefly at the round face of a watch pinned to her uniform.

'Hi... look, I read the list Toby made and I understand what's happened, I mean I don't understand but I know what it says. I don't know how I got here or why I'm here, I don't...' She shakes her head, afraid that she might cry as her eyes grow hot with tears. 'Can you tell me what's going on?' The more she tries to think, the more intense the pounding becomes and she briefly fears a brain tumour, but the list said she's had an MRI and another kind of test and she's fine, fine except for the black dot of lost memory. What does that mean? Amnesia. The list said she had amnesia but she knows who she is and who Toby is and Harper. Don't people with amnesia forget everything including their own names?

'Don't you worry, love, it's okay and I'm going to explain it all,' the nurse says. She pats Katelyn reassuringly on her hand.

'I think she's back,' says Toby. 'Do you think she's back?'

'Where did I go?' asks Katelyn. 'Where have I been?'

TWO

LEAH

It's after three in the morning when Leah hears the ping on her phone, alerting her to an incoming text message. She's waiting for news, asleep in her queen-sized bed that takes up almost the whole bedroom in her small apartment, but not really asleep. She has drifted in and out of strange dreams involving Katelyn and Toby and Harper, one in which Harper asked her why her mummy was dead. She shakes her head at the terrible idea of having to explain to a three-year-old what happened to her mother.

It looks like she's back, like it's over, reads the message and she quickly replies, *Thank God*. There's no point in asking any more questions now. Toby will be speaking to Katelyn and probably a doctor will be called. She can go back to sleep and speak to him in the morning, but she's wide awake now, her heart racing slightly, and she doesn't know if it's from relief or if it's panic at what might happen now.

She pictures her best friend in a hospital bed asking the same questions again and again, every few minutes, and shudders. The whole thing felt surreal and impossible and at one point she was sure that Katelyn must just be playing an elaborate practical joke on all of them, although she wasn't the kind of person to do such a thing.

Will all her memory return now? Will she remember the party and everything that happened at the party?

Climbing out of bed she angles her body so that she can move around to the closet to grab a jumper. It's cold in the apartment without the heater on. In her living room she switches on the small electric heater, not thinking about the cost and not thinking about why she has to worry about money at the moment.

The strange urge to call Aaron and tell him what has happened overwhelms her and she reminds herself again that he is not hers to call anymore. He doesn't deserve to know what has happened to Katelyn anyway. He doesn't deserve to hear from any of them ever again.

The party feels like it was weeks ago, months ago even. So much happened. By midnight she had been sure that her friendship with Katelyn was over, that her whole life had changed forever and then Katelyn just, sort of, blanked. It's the only way Leah can think to describe it to herself. Katelyn blanked.

She had been holding her hands up at the time. 'I don't understand what you're saying,' she said to Toby as Leah watched. They were all in the living room, it was after eleven and they were surrounded by the sad remains of the party, all the guests having left to get home to babysitters. All their friends were in their late thirties and early forties, burdened with large mortgages and young children as they worked towards Instagrammable lives. Parties were always over by 11 p.m., despite everyone vowing to keep going until the early hours of the morning as they all used to do in their twenties.

She and Katelyn and Toby were standing in the living room where silver and white plastic bowls, filled with the remains of salsa, guacamole, chips and peanuts, littered every surface. The vivid chunky red of salsa and brown-green of avocado exposed to air turned Leah's stomach because she had definitely had too much to drink. It was seeing Aaron that had done it.

'Please, I don't understand,' Katelyn said and then she stepped back, her foot landing on a plastic cup lying on the dark timber floor, empty and on its side.

The crack of the cup snapping in half was loud in the silence of the room and Katelyn blinked once and stopped speaking.

Leah sits on the sofa with her phone in her hand rereading the text Toby sent at three o'clock on Sunday morning, after Katelyn had been admitted and Toby had told Leah to go home because only one person was allowed to stay with Katelyn.

They don't think it's a stroke but they are going to do some tests. They've taken blood and they wanted to know how much she had to drink.

Leah had wondered how Toby had answered that question. She had no idea how much any of them had had to drink. It was a party and it was meant to be a lovely celebration. Maybe Katelyn had way too much to drink and that triggered something in her brain, but she hadn't seemed that drunk. Leah knew what she looked like when she was drunk. It never took much to push her over the limit and then she usually got very friendly and quickly, very sleepy. She had seemed perfectly sober, just unable to remember anything for more than a minute and very confused.

What will happen now? Toby has not left Katelyn's side since he took her to the hospital early Sunday morning. He has remained the steadfast loyal husband, sitting next to his wife's bedside as she asked over and again what was happening and why she was in the hospital.

Leah had wanted to go and sit with her during the day on Sunday but Toby told her not to come.

It's too upsetting and they keep taking her away for tests and things. I'll let you know when there's any news.

Yesterday afternoon – Sunday afternoon – there had been news.

They think it's something called transient global amnesia. Apparently, it's caused by stress sometimes. It will resolve itself but she may never remember the party.

Leah wonders what Katelyn will remember, if she ever does, and what will happen now that she seems to have come out of whatever has been going on with her brain.

She's looked up what this is, read stories from people who have suffered from it, and it is caused by stress, or by the shock of the body getting into very cold water, or even by orgasm. It's caused by a lot of things and there isn't much that can be done about the missing memories. For more than twenty-four hours Katelyn has been unable to form new memories or to remember the party. She has, effectively, lost more than a whole day. She has probably lost much more than just time, a lot more. But she doesn't know that.

She had seemed perfectly fine during the party, talking to people, having a good time. She had been fine when they blew out her birthday candles on the three-tier chocolate cake filled with decadent whipped cream. She had seemed fine until everything was over and the three of them were in the living room, tempers frayed and feelings hurt. More than hurt. Destroyed.

Leah will not know how much comes back until she sees Katelyn and only then will she know what she has to do.

THREE

KATELYN AND LEAH – SIX YEARS OLD

Leah hops across the pink chalk-drawn squares on one foot and then turns around and hops back again. The whole school is empty and everything is quiet. She's never been at school this late before. She is practising her hopping in front of the school office while she waits for her mum. It's hot in the afternoon sun and she should be wearing her yellow bucket hat but she doesn't want to because the hat makes her hotter.

Inside the office, Mrs Jackson the school secretary is on the phone. Leah hops forward five times and then turns around again. School feels weird when no one else is there. Well, not no one else. There is another girl. Leah knows her name is Katelyn but they are not in the same class. Katelyn is in Mr Bent's class and Leah is in Mrs Solan's class. Katelyn is sitting on the 'waiting bench', where anyone whose mum is late to fetch them from school gets to sit. Mrs Jackson can see all the children on the waiting bench from her desk. At the end of the day there had been seven children on the waiting bench. Leah counted twice, but now it's just Katelyn because Leah can't sit still anymore.

Leah was sitting on the waiting bench but now she is hopping.

Mrs Jackson comes out of the office and says, 'Leah, love, that was Mum. She says that she's leaving your nana's house now and she will be here very soon.' Leah nods and goes back to hopping. This morning her mum said that she would be late fetching her because Nana was coming home from her hip operation and Mum had to get her settled. 'I don't know what time they're going to release her but you are not to worry, darling. I've told Mrs Jackson and you just sit on the waiting bench until I get there.' Her mum had been very worried about being late and had explained three times that she had to help Nana. She also put two chocolate chip cookies in Leah's lunch box to eat while she waited, but Leah ate them at lunch instead. Her mum makes the best chocolate chip cookies.

'Katelyn,' says Mrs Jackson. 'I'm sorry, love, I can't seem to get hold of your mum at all.' Inside the office, the phone rings and Mrs Jackson hurries away to answer it, puffing and panting. Mrs Jackson looks very hot, even though she is wearing a red sundress. Mum says that February is the hottest month of the year in Sydney and she's right. Leah feels the burn of the sun on the top of her head. Katelyn is wearing her hat so her head is not burning. Leah hops forward and back again.

'Okay,' Katelyn says and nods even though Mrs Jackson is already back in her cool office. Leah sees her wipe her cheek. She's crying. Leah stops hopping and goes to stand near her.

'Where's your mum?' she asks.

Katelyn shrugs but doesn't say anything.

'My mum is never late except for today,' says Leah, feeling that it's important that she explain this. 'My nana hurt her hip but she's better now and on Saturday, I'm going to visit her. Mum said we can bake some cookies to take with us.'

'My mum is always late,' sighs Katelyn.

Leah feels like she needs to do something to stop the little girl being so sad so she sits next to her. 'Want to come and hop with me?' she asks, but Katelyn shakes her head. Katelyn has brown hair and green eyes and her uniform has a big white mark on the front and her hem is all raggedy.

'Oh, Leah, sweetheart,' she hears and looks up to see her mum coming towards her. 'I am so sorry. They let her out so late and then I had to make sure that her carer arrived and you are such a good girl to have waited so patiently.' Leah jumps off the bench and runs to her mother, feeling all warm inside as she gives her a hug and smells the flower perfume her mother sprays in the air in the morning and then walks through. Her mother has blonde hair like she does, but it is cut to her shoulders and swings when she moves her head. But she doesn't have blue eyes like Leah. Leah's eyes are like her dad's eyes.

'I'll grab your bag, love,' says her mother.

Mrs Jackson comes out of the office. 'Um... excuse me, Mrs Randall. Could I have a word?'

'Only a few more minutes, darling,' says her mother as she follows Mrs Jackson back into the office. Leah can see them through the glass doors, talking and nodding at each other.

'I'm going home now,' says Leah and Katelyn nods and rubs her nose with her arm, which Leah is never allowed to do because it's yuck and spreads germs.

When Leah's mum comes back, she is holding Leah's school bag but she is also holding Katelyn's bag.

'Katelyn, your mother just called the office and asked if someone could give you a lift home. Mrs Jackson has an appointment so I'm going to take you. Is that okay?'

Katelyn looks up at Leah's mother and nods. It's not okay but nothing is okay so who cares. Leah's mother is pretty with blonde hair like Leah and brown eyes and she is dressed in fancy clothes.

Katelyn stands up. She's been given a lift home with other people's mothers and fathers lots and lots of times. Once she got a lift home with Jason and his dad and Jason had given her a piece of melted chocolate that made her fingers all sticky.

Leah's mother's car is big and blue and the seats are soft and have a heavy smell. She and Leah sit next to each other and Leah shows her how to put on her seat belt.

'Let me just program this address in,' says Leah's mother, looking down at a piece of paper in her hand. 'We'll have you home in no time.' Katelyn knows her address because she has to say it a lot, she has to say it every time someone gives her a lift home but she keeps quiet, letting the cold air in the car cool her face.

'Why couldn't your mum fetch you?' asks Leah and Katelyn shrugs because she doesn't know how to say it. Her mum was probably having a big sleep and forgot. That happened a lot. She had her cold drink and then she fell asleep.

When they get to the building where Katelyn lives with her mum, she climbs out of the car and says, 'Thank you for the lift,' because that's being polite and she's always polite when people give her a lift home.

'Now just wait there, sweetheart,' says Leah's mother, climbing out of the car and opening the boot. 'I'm going to walk you to your door. Take your bag, there you go.'

Katelyn wants to tell her 'no,' but she can't because you're not allowed to say that to a grown-up.

'Come on, Leah,' says Leah's mum.

Katelyn's apartment is on the third floor and Leah and her mother follow her up the stairs. Katelyn walks slowly, slowly because she doesn't want them to see her sleeping mum. But finally, they are outside her apartment and Leah's mum knocks on the door, once, twice, three times.

'Mum must be busy,' she says, smiling down at Katelyn as they wait, with a big grown-up smile that looks like it's not a real smile at all. Katelyn nods her head. Finally, the door is opened and Katelyn's mum is there. Her hair is messy and she is holding a cold drink in her hand. 'Oh,' she says, 'I thought it was just Katelyn.'

'I didn't want to let her walk up by herself,' says Leah's mum, her smile getting bigger. 'She's such a little thing.'

Her mum looks down at her like she's in big trouble just for being little and then she puts her drink down on a table by the door next to the basket filled with elastic bands and keys and a crumpled tissue. Her mum stands up straight. 'Well, thank you for bringing her home. I had some car trouble. It's much appreciated.' Her voice is high and she doesn't sound like she always does when she says, 'You'll be the death of me, kid.'

'Oh, it's a pleasure,' says Leah's mum. 'No problem at all.' And then she smiles again and Katelyn can see her look behind her mum where the sofa is piled up with blankets because her mum likes to sleep on the sofa during the day and she doesn't care how hot it is.

'Yes, well,' says Katelyn's mum, 'you know how hard it is to find a good mechanic.' She rubs her head. 'And, of course, I have a terrible headache, the heat, you know.' Her mum is dressed in the same pyjama pants she was wearing this morning when she dropped her off at school and her hair is all scrunched up and there is black stuff under her eyes like there was this morning as well. Katelyn recognises the funny medicine smell that's always on her when she hasn't showered. She wishes that Leah and her mum were not standing right there.

'Oh, I know, the heat is dreadful,' says Leah's mum softly and she sounds sad. 'Maybe Katelyn could come over and spend the rest of the afternoon with us and you can... get your car sorted.'

Katelyn closes her eyes and she hopes and hopes that her

mum says 'yes' because then maybe she and Leah can bake cookies together and she can even eat some. Her tummy is all rumbly because she couldn't find the cheese in the fridge this morning and so she had to just have bread and she hates bread with nothing, so she only ate half a slice and threw the rest away. She looks up at her mother, trying to make her understand how much she wants to go but she knows better than to say anything. Sometimes saying things got her a 'quick slap on the ear'.

Her mother is quiet for a long, long time. 'If not that's fine,' says Leah's mum.

'No, of course it's okay,' her mum says. 'It would be lovely for Katelyn. She's new to the school. We just moved last month and things are very hectic, as you can imagine. It's so hard being a single mother as well... my ex is really not interested in raising his child at all.' Her mother laughs like it's funny but Katelyn knows it's not funny. Her mum is talking too much and too fast.

Leah's mum leans forward and touches her mum on the arm. 'Katelyn can come home with us and maybe even stay the night. I can get her to school and then you can have some time to yourself.'

'Aren't you kind,' says Katelyn's mum. 'That would be lovely. I'll just grab some of her...' Her mum looks around like she's trying to remember what Katelyn needs.

'Maybe a toothbrush and some pyjamas and clean underwear,' says Leah's mum and Katelyn feels her face get hot and her eyes burn because a mum should know what to get. She looks down at her shoes which have a big scratch on them.

'Yes, give me a moment,' says her mum and then she closes the door and doesn't even say, 'Would you like to come in for a cup of tea?' but Katelyn knows that only mothers on television do that and when they do their houses are neat and clean and not a pile of boxes and lots of cold drink that smells funny and Katelyn can't have.

'A sleepover will be fun, won't it?' Leah's mum says to her, smiling wide, and Leah nods because sleepovers are always fun even though she usually only has them at her nana's house.

'Can she sleep in my room?' she asks her mum. She and Katelyn haven't played together at lunch or anything but that doesn't matter. Tomorrow when she goes back to school, she'll be able to tell Anita and Emma that she had a sleepover just like the girls in the chapter book Mrs Solan is reading to them in class.

'Of course she can sleep in your room, sweetheart,' says her mother.

'You can see my room and I even have an under bed for you,' she says to Katelyn because Katelyn looks sad about the sleepover, or maybe she's just sad about everything. Katelyn's mum is not like any other mum Leah knows. Her eyes are red and her hair is messy and she doesn't smell like flowers.

When Katelyn's mum comes back she is holding a yucky plastic bag with some things for Katelyn and she gives it to Leah's mum saying, 'You behave, young lady,' and they go down to the car again. When Leah sleeps over at her nana's house, she takes a small pink backpack with everything she needs, including sleepy teddy who always helps her close her eyes.

'Do you have a sleepy teddy?' she asks Katelyn when they are buckled into their seats.

'No,' says Katelyn. 'What's a sleepy teddy?'

'I'll show you at home,' says Leah, excited about having someone sleep in her room for the first time.

That night Katelyn sleeps on the under bed on the floor of Leah's room and she has the best sleep ever because she has eaten three cookies and special home-made chicken nuggets for dinner and Leah's mum has even fixed her raggedy hem and she wishes, wishes that she could live at Leah's house forever. She and Leah have played with her doll's house and her Barbie dolls and her paints and she knows who sleepy teddy is now and Leah even has a cat with soft ears.

Just before she falls asleep, she hears Leah whisper, 'You're the first person I've ever had for a sleepover so now we have to be best friends.'

'Forever?' asks Katelyn, because more than anything in the world she wants a forever best friend, a forever person.

'Of course,' says Leah. 'We'll be best friends forever. We'll never fight and we'll always love each other.'

'Always,' agrees Katelyn. 'Always.'

FOUR

Leah watches as Toby turns up the music and then takes another swig of his beer. Everyone who has arrived has headed immediately for the drinks table, as though they have only recently been released from prison and need to get drunk as quickly as possible, which she supposes the parents of young children sometimes feel is the truth.

She's halfway through a plastic cup filled with a bright-pink raspberry slushie doctored with a little more vodka than was already added to give her a buzz.

She's watching the door in between helping Katelyn make sure everyone has a drink.

'Don't you look sexy,' a man says as he comes up to the table where Leah is standing, crouching down and getting himself a drink from a silver tub filled with ice and a selection of beers.

Leah smiles, cocks her head to the side and pulls her shoulders back slightly. The silver top plunges in the front and her white jeans are second-skin tight.

'Oh, hey, honey, grab me a drink,' a woman calls from across the room and the man with compliments on the tip of his tongue stands and smiles.

'The wife,' he says, shrugging, and then he grabs a plastic cup to take to the whirling cocktail slushie machine.

Leah sighs. She didn't even get a chance to ask him his name. His child is probably at school with Harper. The whole place is filled with preschool mothers and their husbands, people from an entirely different world from Leah's world and people in whose conversations she has to feign interest constantly.

The house does look amazing. The Winter Wonderland theme had been a good idea with winter roaring into Sydney next month. A white and silver extravaganza, was how Katelyn had explained the party she wanted to have for her thirty-sixth birthday. 'Everyone has to dress in those colours,' she said glee-fully. Katelyn herself is dressed in fitted black jeans and a gorgeous silver silk top.

She's gone all the way, filling the house with silver snowflakes and silver tinsel, white tablecloths on all the tables and even one draped on the sofa. Fairy lights look like stars in snow and translucent LED balloons are everywhere. The stuff she bought is over the top and clichéd, like her silly party invitation, but it looks beautiful. The buffet table is littered with tiny decorative snowflakes and polystyrene balls glued together, symbolising snow. The caterer has provided all Kate-lyn's favourite foods – delicious tacos filled with fish or beef, or beans for the vegetarians. Platters of cheese and vegetables and giant plates of nachos drizzled with bright red salsa and smothered in melted cheese are everywhere. Leah has seen the selection of desserts in the kitchen where chocolate is king.

Red and white wine, bottles of tequila, vodka, whisky and gin line the drinks table. A slushie machine whirls, waiting for people to dispense their own slushie cocktails, and loud music from Katelyn's playlist, filled with all her favourite songs from when she was sixteen, thumps through the air.

Leah straightens some cups on the drinks table and then she looks up and sees Aaron.

He is standing by the front door, talking to someone with his back to her, but it can only be Aaron with his military-style haircut, leaving him with a short covering of grey-black hair, and his broad shoulders and tight black shirt. He still has the power to make her heart skip.

Instead of saying 'hello', like she should do as an evolved adult, she leaves the room and goes into the kitchen where Katelyn is pouring corn chips into a bowl to go with the guacamole she has mixed up.

'You okay?' Katelyn asks without looking at Leah, as she concentrates on opening another bag of chips, putting one into her mouth and crunching it as she works.

'Sure,' says Leah, grabbing a handful of chips for herself, letting the salty taste of the corn distract her. *Why did you have to invite him? Why did he have to be here? We're divorced and I should never have to see him again. Why aren't you on my side?* Keeping her thoughts to herself, Leah dips a chip in the bright green guacamole studded with tomatoes. 'Delicious,' she says after shoving the chip in her mouth.

'Good,' says Katelyn, distracted as she looks around the kitchen for anything she may have forgotten. 'What was I doing?' she says and Leah laughs.

'Getting drunk, I imagine.'

'Yes,' agrees Katelyn with a smile. 'Getting drunk.'

'I'll finish up in here, you go and say hello to your guests,' says Leah.

'Yes, guests,' says Katelyn.

'Stay away from the drinks table,' says Leah, concerned that Katelyn has had way too much already.

'Okay,' says Katelyn agreeably and she leaves, walking into the living room where a chorus of 'Happy birthdays' greets her.

If Leah had a party tomorrow, she would not be able to fill a room half the size of Katelyn's living room. Her life is her work and now that she is divorced, little else. Her world has contracted as Katelyn's has expanded to include mothers' groups and preschool and literally anyone who has a child.

Leah wants to be able to walk out into the party and blend in, but she knows she stands out. She has always stood out but it is only lately that she has not enjoyed the feeling.

You're an adult, go talk to him, she tells herself and squaring her shoulders she flips her hair away from her neck and goes to find her ex-husband. She looks good tonight and at least he'll know what he's missing. That's the best she can hope for, that her ex-husband regrets their divorce. It will have to be enough for tonight.

The song changes and Leah sings along to All the Things She Said, thinking of everything she would like to say to Aaron. She'll just say 'hello', that's all. Nothing else needs to be said.

Not yet.

FIVE

KATELYN

Monday, 2 p.m. - Two Days After the Party

'Are you okay there?' asks Toby as she walks through the front door and Katelyn grits her teeth at the question. He is treating her as though she is infirm, and she's not. Physically, she's fine.

She cannot remember the party, the entire party. The fact that she can't remember her time in hospital, the whole of Sunday, doesn't bother her as much as not remembering the party that she had planned for and shopped for. She is dressed in the clothes she wore for the party because that's all she had at the hospital. Toby hadn't thought to go home and get something else for her to wear so she had struggled into her black jeans and the beautiful, but stained, silver top when they said it was fine for her to go home. She feels ridiculous and uncomfortable.

'Did anything happen during that time, something that may have triggered this?' Amanda, the nurse taking care of her, had asked Toby when they had ascertained that she was cognisant of the day and time and that she had remembered details like the date of her birthday and who the prime minister of Australia was, that she was, as Toby said, 'back'.

'No, nothing, it was just a party,' Toby said. 'Everyone had fun and left reasonably early because everyone has kids.'

Katelyn had been sitting up in her hospital bed, desperately trying to break through the black wall that was keeping her from her memories of at least twenty-four hours, so she wasn't really listening to what Toby was saying but she did hear his tone. And she knows he's lying. When Toby is lying, his voice gets a little higher. It's subtle and not something most people notice. You have to know Toby really well to pick up on it. She identified the trait when they were dating and at a restaurant. Toby had ordered his steak done medium and it had been brought to him overdone, grey and tough.

'Complain,' Katelyn said. 'Send it back.' But Toby had looked around the small restaurant crammed with diners and seen that there was only one waitress serving everyone, looking harassed as she ran between tables and kept apologising to guests for making them wait. 'It's fine,' he said. 'I'll just eat it.'

When the waitress came to give them their bill, she asked how everything was and Toby said, 'Very good, thanks,' his voice a whole tone higher, making Katelyn laugh, even though Toby didn't understand what she was laughing at.

The slight rising of his tone when he's lying is not something he's even aware of and not something she would tell him. She likes knowing when he's lying, likes knowing that she needs to keep questioning him should she need to, but the truth is that Toby rarely lies to her. There's simply no reason. She's heard the tone out in the world when he's trying to spare people's feelings, but she's only heard it once or twice in their marriage when he is talking to her.

'Does this dress make me look old and frumpy?' she asked him last year when she was choosing something to wear to a friend's Christmas party.

'No, of course not,' he said, his voice rising slightly.

'Really, it's fine if it does, I just wanted to make sure,' Katelyn said.

'Well, it's very frilly,' Toby replied, his tone dropping as he told the truth and Katelyn took off the dress and pushed it to the back of her wardrobe. Part of her was relieved she could access this memory as she sat in the hospital bed. But she was also alarmed as she wondered what her husband was hiding from her.

He's never had a reason to lie to her before, or at least to keep lying, but hearing him speak to Amanda, Katelyn knew he was lying about the party.

Something happened at the party. Something Toby doesn't want to discuss.

She wanted to ask him what it was in the car but she is exhausted, which feels impossible since she spent a lot of time sleeping, according to Toby. She's glad to be home and as soon as she's rested, she will ask him what he's keeping from her. It can't be anything major. Maybe she got really drunk and embarrassed herself, although the nurse didn't say anything about how much alcohol she'd had. If Toby won't explain things, she knows Leah will.

'Are you all right?' Toby asks again and Katelyn sighs.

'I'm fine,' she says, making her way through to the living room where there is nothing but chaos.

'Sorry, I would have tidied up but...' says Toby.

'It's okay, what time did your mum say she was bringing Harper home?'

'Um... I thought maybe it would be better if Harper stayed with her another night, but I can call her, whatever you want.' Katelyn hates that Toby is being so accommodating, is treating her like one wrong word will catapult her back into amnesia. Would it? She knows so little about what happened to her. If she had the energy, she would already have looked up everything there was to know about what happened to her but she feels weak and strange.

'Once the TGA has resolved itself, there doesn't seem to be a risk of a reoccurrence but you may want to limit stress over the next few days,' the neurologist, a woman with long black hair and thick, dark eyebrows, told her. 'I would also recommend that you stay away from alcohol and any kind of drugs,' she said. 'But as far as we can see, there are no underlying heart conditions or anything like that. That's what we worry about when something like this happens and you are perfectly healthy. We're just waiting for some blood tests to come back but I think it's fine for you to go home.'

Katelyn had nodded as she spoke, listening but not listening as she tried to search her mind for the missing hours. Moments from the party seem to come back to her but then just disappear, so she has to question if she really remembers anything about it at all, or if she is just imagining things.

'You were fine until after eleven at least,' Toby told her as they walked to his car to drive home.

She had seemed fine but she wasn't. She was at the party, talking to people and eating and drinking, but her brain had been somewhere else entirely. It was a surreal and frightening thought – the idea that who she was could just disappear for some time.

'And what happened then?' she asked.

'Nothing, it was... everyone was gone by then and we were just starting to clean up. Leah was there and we were talking and then you just seemed to forget what you were saying and then you started repeating yourself and asking the same questions over and again and we had no idea what was wrong with you.'

Looking around her living room, Katelyn wishes she could remember one thing, just one thing, because maybe that would lead to everything else. Toby has returned her phone and she has scrolled through the text messages that have come in all day thanking her for the celebration.

Thanks so much for having us, everything was fabulous, loved your outfit!

Thanks for having us, food was divine and you looked amazing. Happy Birthday again!

Thanks for the great party – everything was wonderful, hope to see you next week at the preschool drinks evening xx

She has no memory at all of the whole of Sunday when she was in the hospital, but she thought that the time before would instantly return and it hasn't.

At least people seemed to have had a good time. She bends down and starts picking up plastic plates from the floor, stepping on a plastic cup and hearing the crack under her foot and feeling a shooting pain in her head. She raises her hand to touch her temple. 'Let me do it,' says Toby. 'You just go upstairs and lie down.'

'Stop hovering, Toby, I'm fine and I need to move a little. I've been lying down for a whole day.'

Toby goes to the kitchen and returns with a garbage bag. 'There are a lot of presents in the study for you to open, but you said you wanted to wait until Harper got home so she could open them with you.'

'Are you sure she's okay with your mum for another night? She's never slept over for two nights before.'

'Mum says she's fine and I spoke to her and she was actually quite excited. You know Mum and Dad, they let her run the show.'

Katelyn nods. She is grateful to have Maureen and Ted in her life, grateful they are there when they are needed and that they are able to share in the joy of raising Harper. Would her mother have bonded with her only grandchild or would she have been as dismissive and disinterested as she was in her own daughter? *You're more like her than you ever wanted to be.*

Katelyn sighs – she's not going to think about her mother today of all days. She begins gathering up a collection of half-empty dip bowls, wrinkling her nose at the stale smell. 'Can you ask your mum to drop her at preschool tomorrow and then I'll fetch her?' She wants to see her daughter but she also knows she would benefit from some rest and time to clean up the house, digest what's happened to her and find a way to put it into some kind of perspective. She's struggling with that right now and Toby keeps talking and the 'thank you' texts keep coming in and what she would like most is to just be left alone so she can think this through on her own.

She grabs a handful of the silver plastic snowflakes from the dining room table, chucking them in the garbage bag she is holding and has a flash of how the room looked when she was finished setting up on Saturday evening.

She had been working on the house all day and she was tired, more tired than she believed possible but when she was done, Toby had dimmed the lights and put on some music and for a few minutes she felt in the mood to celebrate as the LED balloons shone and the fairy lights blinked like stars.

'I remember before the party,' she says to Toby. 'I remember how the room looked and that I was tired.'

'And after that?' he asks, hopeful and yet guarded at the same time.

Katelyn closes her eyes. 'Nothing,' she says. 'Nothing.' She shakes her head and then swallows. She's not going to cry.

What happened to make her lose her memory? She's only thirty-six. Is this a sign of things to come? Could it happen again? Will she find herself being diagnosed with Alzheimer's or dementia in the next decade? The doctor had patiently answered all her questions at the hospital, but Katelyn is not sure she can believe her. What if she was lying just to keep Katelyn calm? Is that possible? Did doctors do that?

Once the garbage bag is filled, she takes it into the kitchen, thirsty for some water. Toby is loading the dishwasher with platters, scraping off cheese that has become glue over two days and throwing away congealed tacos that smell like they're already rotting.

Her phone pings, and she sighs, pulling it out of her pocket to read the latest message.

'You should just turn it off,' says Toby. 'You can respond to everyone tomorrow.'

'You haven't told anyone, have you?' Alarm flares inside her at the thought of her memory loss becoming fodder for the whole preschool and all their other friends. She hates being talked about.

'No, just Leah, obviously, because she was here, and Mum and Dad, but I thought you could decide if you wanted to share it when you were ready. Just put it on silent if you don't want to turn it off.'

'Yes,' says Katelyn, her eyes moving over the words in the text. 'Yes, I will but I'm just going to… the bathroom,' she says, dropping the bag on the kitchen floor.

In her bathroom she sits down on the edge of the bathtub and reads the message again.

I'm so, so sorry about everything that happened at the party and I'm here to talk. You know where to find me when you're ready.

The message is from Aaron. Leah's ex-husband. Why? What happened at the party? And why would Aaron be contacting her about it?

SIX

LEAH

She takes her time getting dressed because she has all the time in the world. When she's done, she looks at her bank balance again. She should never have offered to pay for lunch with Katelyn last week, but it was her turn.

She could go to her parents to ask for money but she can just see her mother shaking her head at her. 'Really, Leah? How often have Dad and I had the "living beyond your means" conversation? Katelyn managed all her life on so very little, surely you can manage on your large salary?' And that would lead to the conversation that she wasn't ready to have with anyone. Leah has an older brother who lives in the US. He's a scientist and mostly distracted and obsessed with his work in neurological disease research. From years of conversations with different friends, Leah knows that being compared to a smarter or more successful sibling is something a lot of people struggle with. But her brother, Tom, is seven years older than her and she has never been compared to him in any way. Instead, since they became friends at six years old, her mother has, without thinking, used Katelyn as a metric for the right way to do things. Katelyn doesn't have a job right now because Harper is still so little, but Leah has no doubt that if she did have a job, she would certainly never have to deal with the ignominy of being fired.

As far as everyone close to her is concerned, she is still employed at We Adore You cosmetics. She has yet to tell anyone she's been fired for getting, as her twenty-eight-year-old boss told her, 'Just so flaky.' Brooke lived up to her name in that she looked like she had stepped straight out of hair and make-up for some soap opera, with her porcelain-smooth skin and her almost waist-length chestnut hair that sat perfectly all day. She had over one hundred thousand followers on Instagram and more on TikTok and was, according to everyone, very much part of the wave of future marketing executives.

Leah hadn't even minded when she was hired a year and a half ago because she was leading the team and she had hired her. She bites down on her lip a little too hard, letting the physical pain distract her from the mental anguish that fact causes her. She had actually hired Brooke.

'You better watch out for that one,' her second in charge, Jordan, said at the time. 'She has her eyes on your job.' Leah had laughed off his remarks, not because she didn't see Brooke's ambition but because she didn't care. At the time, she had been completely secure in her position and her plans for her future. When Jordan left to take another job, Leah had happily promoted Brooke into his position.

A year ago, she had been planning to fall pregnant and leave work behind to raise a child. All she had been waiting for was the right time, the time when Aaron would finally accept that he loved her enough to want a child with her.

Instead, she got divorced. In public she has been sanguine, telling everyone, 'We're just two different people now to who we were a few years ago. I wish him everything of the best, I really do.' But alone, in her one-bedroom apartment that she had signed a lease on without even viewing, she has been slowly falling apart. And that led to mistakes at work. One mistake was forgiven and understood. She was getting divorced. Everyone in her team, even Brooke, had been solicitous, bringing her gifts of coffee and soothing words. The CEO had called from Hong Kong and Leah had somehow survived the humiliation of a conversation where she accepted taking a step back and letting Brooke lead the team so that she could, as Brooke said in the conference call, 'Really focus on yourself,' her voice oozing concern.

Leah had swallowed the demotion and vowed to take back her position as team leader, but somehow she couldn't seem to regain her focus.

A second and third mistake and even one where she called a supplier 'a bitch' for refusing to give their website exclusivity was waved away.

Her fury at the time had not been towards the supplier, who was simply making an economical decision, but towards Aaron. She had just read a text from her lawyer telling her that Aaron had never put her name on the beautiful three-bedroom apartment with ocean views they had shared for three years. The supplier explaining that they didn't want to restrict themselves to just one website had simply been on a call with Leah at the wrong time.

'I'm just so shocked you would do such a thing, Leah,' Brooke had said, after pulling Leah into her bubblegum candle-scented office where a huge bouquet of roses from Brooke's fiancé stood on the desk in a glass vase.

'I'm so sorry,' Leah replied, hanging her head so Brooke wouldn't see how humiliated she was by her lapse. 'Things are just so hard at the moment.' She hated how whiny she sounded, knowing that if she had an employee like herself, she would be horrified.

'Of course they are,' Brooke said, patting Leah on the shoulder. 'It must be terribly hard to go through what you're going through.'

Nodding, Leah had looked up at her young boss. 'Thank you for understanding.'

'Absolutely,' said Brooke, 'but let's try to not let anything like that happen again.' She smiled, her voice chipper with encouragement for Leah to do better.

And then Leah made a mistake that couldn't be forgiven. While trying to load a new product she mistakenly deleted half the images on the website. She was hungover after a night of feeling sorry for herself and had somehow clicked on pages of images and then pressed the 'delete all' button. She knew it was the last straw and she didn't even wait for the letter telling her she was fired. She just picked up everything from her desk and walked out, hoping that she had reached rock bottom and that things would start to get better. They didn't.

Once she's dressed, she sits on her sofa and opens her computer to check in on all her job applications. Her experience in cosmetic marketing can translate to anything but it feels as though the whole of Sydney is talking about her spectacular meltdown, and every time she applies for something, she can almost see the HR person reading her application and saying, 'Isn't she the one who deleted half a website?'

Her phone clicks with a text coming in, the sound irritating her because she has a special tone for replies to her job applications and the clicking is just an ordinary text.

We're home. She seems okay. Not sure what I should tell her or if I should tell her anything at all. Maybe it's better to just let it all go.

Leah allows herself a bitter laugh. How very like Toby, how very sweet and kind and loyal of him to want to do that for Katelyn. She is, after all, the mother of his child. What power a woman has over a man when they are connected by a child, how easy it is for her to hold onto him. Leah knows that people would dispute that with her but right now it's her experience. She and Aaron had no children together and were as easily separated as a hot knife runs through butter. And despite paying her share of household bills, she and Aaron didn't even own a property together, so his refusal to sell his apartment would have meant hours in court and thousands of dollars in legal fees if she wanted to fight for her share. So she's in a rental unit and now she's unemployed. And Toby, lovely Toby, who had been her one bright spark in all this, wants to 'just let it all go'.

She drops her computer back onto the sofa and goes into the bathroom, opening the bottom drawer and staring down. The word is still there on the blue and white plastic test, even after three days. PREGNANT. Toby has no idea about the test. Not yet.

Leah shoves the drawer closed, slamming it hard as she bursts into tears. How can this have happened? How on earth can this have happened?

Katelyn is home now, probably cleaning up after the party with her husband by her side. She knows Harper is with Maureen and Ted and even though she called Maureen and offered to take Harper for a day, her offer was politely refused. 'Ted and I are happy to have her as long as she needs to stay,' said Maureen, who reminds Leah of her own mother, Teresa. Both women are in their sixties and both women have enjoyed long, wonderful marriages and even managed to have their own careers when their children were older. Maureen went back to university to become a psychologist and Leah's mother had taken up floristry and now owns a very successful store. Two women from a generation where it was more difficult to combine motherhood and a career and yet both of them have succeeded. And here was Leah with every single advantage and no child and no career. She cannot fathom how her life has spiralled out of control so fast.

She reads Toby's text again, thinking about the way he had looked at her when she arrived at the party.

'Hey, don't you look beautiful,' he said, when he opened the door to her. She had smiled and stepped forward, kissing him on the cheek as she always did, catching the scent of his sandalwood aftershave.

'You look pretty fab yourself,' she said because he did, the beautiful white shirt he was wearing accentuating his dark-brown eyes. She and Katelyn had chosen the shirt together, Katelyn saying, 'You have such fabulous taste and you always know what looks good on him,' as they wandered through a department store after their usual midweek lunch.

'He'll love this,' Leah said, lifting the crisp white shirt with silver detailing on the cuffs off the rail.

'Really? Isn't it a bit bright for him?' asked Katelyn, wrinkling her nose.

'No, it'll be perfect,' Leah replied and it was.

She had dressed carefully for the party, knowing that it would be filled with couples, many of whom had heard about her divorce. She hadn't seen some of them for ages but she wanted the women to envy her and the men to be attracted to her. She had bought a metallic silver top that plunged in the front and teamed it with skintight white jeans. Her hair was perfectly straight and her lipstick cherry red.

'You look so sexy,' said Katelyn when Leah found her in the kitchen, refilling ice trays.

'You look amazing, Kate,' she replied because Katelyn did look wonderful. Her chestnut hair curled loosely around her face and her silver silk top clung in all the right places. 'Love the smoky eye shadow.'

Katelyn had reached up to touch her eye lightly as though she didn't know that she had covered her lids in shadowed grey and silver and lined them in black.

'Where's Harper?' Leah asked. Katelyn had looked around the kitchen as if expecting to see her daughter standing right there. 'Has Maureen already picked her up?'

'Yes, yes,' Katelyn agreed.

'Aw, I wanted to see her, but I'll have the whole night with her next weekend when you and Toby have your date night,' said Leah.

'Yes,' agreed Katelyn, but she looked like she had forgotten the date. 'How's work?'

'Fine, fine, good,' replied Leah, swallowing some of the guilt at the secret she was keeping. She had no job and the days yawned before her.

'Thirty-six, can you believe it?' asked Leah.

'I can't, I don't feel like I'm thirty-six until Harper wakes me at 6 a.m., then I feel like I'm five hundred.'

'You're so lucky, Kate, you really have it all.' Leah felt her eyes fill and blinked quickly.

'We both do, come on, no getting sentimental now.'

As she said the words the doorbell rang and Toby called, 'I'll get it,' and the party had begun.

'You look so sexy,' Katelyn said again and Leah laughed. She had assumed that Katelyn was just making the point again, but maybe that was the start of whatever happened with her memory.

By the time the party ended Leah understood that Katelyn didn't just have it all. She wanted it all: no matter who got hurt in the process. And that's fine because Leah is more than capable of doing a little hurting of her own. Leah wants it all too. On the way to the hospital, she had been concerned for her friend, had been consoling her all the way, but she kept thinking, *Isn't this convenient? Isn't this really convenient?*

You couldn't blame someone for their terrible behaviour if they didn't remember it.

But if Katelyn did remember then who would she blame for what happened? Would she remember what Leah told her? Would that terrible truth be something that comes back to Katelyn? Leah shivers, dreading the idea of that possibility.

'I can't remember,' Katelyn kept saying on the drive to the hospital. 'I want to remember.'

Katelyn wants to remember what happened at the party and Toby just wants to forget everything and, sitting on her sofa, Leah realises that what happens now is completely up to her. She hasn't felt that way for some time and she likes the feeling very much. Right now, she has the power to change things for all of them.

Her phone pings and seeing it's from one of her job applications she opens it quickly, her eyes scanning the form rejection email.

Unable to contain her fury she flings her phone across the room, experiencing a wave of relief when it lands unbroken on the carpet. She can't afford a new phone.

Dragging her body off the sofa a plan begins to take shape. She knows exactly what she's going to do and she doesn't care who gets hurt in the process. It can't be acceptable that she's the only one who gets hurt. Not anymore.

SEVEN

KATELYN AND LEAH – SIXTEEN YEARS OLD

Katelyn stands by the school gate, looking down at her copy of *Macbeth*, the play she is supposed to be reading for English but she's not really reading it at all. She read it before the school term started, assuming that everyone else in the class would do the same thing but they haven't and now their English teacher is making them read aloud some parts and Katelyn is so completely bored. The February sun overhead beats down, making her itchy and hot, and she sighs.

Instead of reading, she is surreptitiously watching Leah meld her body into Jason Elland's giant form. The two locked lips five minutes ago and haven't come up for air. Katelyn is waiting for Leah so they can catch the bus home to Leah's house and do their homework together, even though they are not in the same classes or even studying the same things.

She goes home with Leah most afternoons. It's better than going home to her apartment where her mother will be either in the middle of a bender or in the middle of furious sobriety. Neither of those states is pleasant to be around. In the ten years she has known Leah, Katelyn has come to think of the Randall household as home. Teresa, Leah's mum, is probably one of the best people Katelyn knows, aside from Leah. From the first sleepover, Teresa has treated her like a daughter, making sure she has lunch for school every day by sending extra with Leah, making sure her uniform looks right and in some cases buying her new stuff, making sure she feels that she has someone she can talk to. Because she has needed someone to talk to her whole life. Sometimes she and Teresa will start talking about stuff like books they both like and Leah will get bored and just go up to her room, leaving the two of them together, and those are the best times because that's when Katelyn pretends that Teresa really is her mother, not that she would ever tell Leah that. Leah's older brother, Tom, treats her exactly the same way he treats Leah – as though she's a vaguely interesting alien creature.

'Hey,' he says when he sees her and then he studies her for a moment and ignores her for the rest of the time. When Katelyn sleeps over at Leah's house, which is most Saturday nights, she thinks about what it would be like to kiss Tom who is twenty-three and has the same blonde hair and blue eyes Leah does. She has imagined marrying Tom and becoming part of the Randall family forever. She would never tell Leah this because Leah would only laugh at her. She's not really attracted to Tom, more like she's attracted to the idea of being part of his family.

A fantasy she has never shared with anyone is the one of her coming home one day to find her mother dead and then having to move in with Leah permanently. She used to feel bad about the fantasy until last year when her mother went on another bender and woke her up one morning by throwing an empty carton of orange juice at her head and calling her a 'whore'.

'We're out of orange juice because you finished the last drop and didn't replace it, stupid whore,' were the exact words her mother used, or slurred. She liked to mix orange juice with her vodka for breakfast. And then she had lobbed the empty carton at Katelyn's head, where a cardboard corner caught her cheek-bone and left a small bloody nick.

'I wish you were dead,' Katelyn had screamed and her mother had laughed.

'I wish you'd never been born. Your existence ruined my life.' When she got sober about a week later, she apologised. Katelyn barely listened. Her mother's apology list was long and complicated and sometimes she told Katelyn she was sorry for something and when Katelyn had no idea what she was talking about, she realised that she had simply dismissed the incident from her mind. It was easier to do that than to hang onto each painful episode, letting it injure her again as she thought about it. She wasn't going to forget the orange juice carton though.

'Please tell me you forgive me,' her mother had begged, forcing Katelyn to say that she did when she didn't.

'It will never happen again. I'm going to stick with it this time,' her mother explained with a smile and Katelyn nodded like she agreed, but she knew her mother was incapable of sticking with it. She'd learned that lesson eventually.

Now she was just waiting to be old enough to leave or for her mother to die. Katelyn knows this makes her a bad person but so what. She's a bad person for a reason.

The other persistent fantasy she has is that Jason Elland – captain of the rugby team and the most beautiful boy on earth with sandy-brown hair and big caramel-coloured eyes and the stubble that's always there no matter how many times the teachers tell him to shave – will one day look at her and want to be with her. She knows she's pretty enough. Her long chestnut hair curls nicely around her shoulders when she leaves it down and her green eyes look good with dark make-up and she can wear pretty much whatever she wants, but she is nothing compared to the Barbie-doll-like goddess that Leah is. Every time Leah goes anywhere in their school, the eyes of the straight male population of the school follow her. Jason Elland is never going to look at Katelyn beyond nodding at her and mumbling, 'Hi,' when he comes up to talk to Leah.

Katelyn's mother is currently sober which means that she spends her day furiously cleaning the apartment and smoking on the balcony, trying to stop her hands from shaking. When Katelyn gets home, she pounces on her, as though she's been waiting for her the whole day.

'How was your day, darling? What did you learn? What did you eat? Look what I made? I went to my meeting. What shall we do for dinner? Want to go for a walk? Want to watch television? Do you have homework? Let me help.'

The first time her mother embraced sobriety was when Katelyn was seven and she assumed her whole world had changed for good. She doesn't think she's ever been as happy as she was for those three months when she thought she had a 'mum just like other mums'. But then her mother slipped back into her bottle of vodka and she was gone again, not caring where Katelyn was or what she was doing. The cycle has gone on for years and last month when her mother told her, 'That's it. I'm done with this crap. I'm never taking another drink,' Katelyn had to stop herself from rolling her eyes.

When her mother is sober, she confesses terrible things to Katelyn that no child should ever have to hear. She talks about her own parents abusing her and the boyfriend who assaulted her and living on the street when she was pregnant with Katelyn before she got help from the government. She keeps repeating the phrase, 'I'm trying, I really am,' which Katelyn thinks is designed to make Katelyn feel sorry for her, but after so many years of the same thing, she has little sympathy for her mother. She's done with forgiveness and understanding.

Looking down at her book again, she watches the letters dance on the page as she feels her eyes heavy with unshed tears. *Stop feeling sorry for yourself*, she commands silently.

'I'll be a minute, I just need to say goodbye,' Leah told her when they met up after class, but it's been fifteen minutes already. Jason doesn't want to let go of Leah for a second. Katelyn knows she should just concentrate on getting her HSC and getting into university so that she can finally get away from her mother, but the ache inside her whenever she sees Jason and Leah is so strong it takes her breath away.

'Right, sorry,' she hears and she looks up, blinking rapidly. 'He didn't want to say goodbye.'

'You two are so cute together.' Katelyn smiles and she hopes Leah can only hear sincerity in her voice.

'We need to run or we'll miss the bus,' says Leah and so Katelyn runs with her and when they make it on to the bus in time they are both laughing so hard Katelyn feels like she can't breathe, and it's the best feeling in the whole world. Joy bubbles inside her because she knows that Teresa will be home and she will ask Katelyn about her *Macbeth* essay as she makes up plates of fruit and vegetables for both girls. And later she and Leah will take a bag of pretzels upstairs with them to finish their homework before dinner but they will spend most of that time discussing everyone at school and giggling about their weird teachers. She will only need to go home much later when her mother is hopefully asleep and right now, that's the best Katelyn can hope for.

Leah stares out of the window as the bus pulls away from the kerb. Truthfully, she wouldn't mind an afternoon alone. Katelyn seems to be over at her house every day but every time she thinks about saying anything, something stops her. 'Can you imagine how difficult life is for her?' her mother asks her when they talk about Katelyn. 'She never knows how her mother is going to behave from one day to the next. I feel so sorry for the poor girl.' And then Leah feels guilty for even thinking about asking Katelyn to give her an afternoon alone.

When they get home, Katelyn will spend at least half an hour talking to her mother about everything she did at school today, discussing her projects and even announcing her grades. Leah's mother is always so proud of her, so supportive. Nothing Leah herself does can ever compete with everything that Katelyn is achieving at school. She's definitely going to be head prefect next year, definitely going to top the year and she definitely has, as every teacher says, 'a very bright future'.

No one says those things about Leah. Leah is beautiful and brilliant at netball, but not brilliant enough to play for Australia. She has Jason and he's lovely, but she would like to confess to Katelyn that he's actually a bit boring to talk to since he mostly cares about sport, any kind of sport. He can discuss rugby and every rugby team in Australia for hours. And sex. He really cares about sex and it's not that she doesn't, but sometimes she just wants to relax and watch a movie on the sofa at his house without him pawing at her the whole time. But he is the most popular boy at school and she is the most popular girl at school, although she doesn't see much of her other friends because not all of them like Katelyn but everyone seems to understand that she and Katelyn are a package deal and Leah doesn't remember signing up for that.

If she and Katelyn had not been friends for so many years, and if Katelyn came from a stable home and Leah never had to feel sorry for her, Leah thinks they probably wouldn't be friends now. But part of her also loves Katelyn, who knows everything there is to know about her and who helps her with her homework and laughs at her stupid jokes and envies her for being with Jason. Leah knows that. It's probably why she's still with Jason, but it makes her feel like a bad person. It's not her fault that Katelyn's mum is a psycho. Leah hates that her own mum loves Katelyn so much and always seems interested in talking to her.

'Come on, dreamy, this is our stop,' says Katelyn as the bus slows down.

'I failed my maths exam, Mum's going to go mad,' says Leah, voicing the one thing she has been really worrying about all day.

'Gawd,' says Katelyn as they both stand up. 'Don't worry, I'll tell her that I only just passed because it was so hard. She'll go easy on you and I can go over it with you and show you what you did wrong.'

Leah smiles. Katelyn is her best friend and she knows that a real best friend is hard to find. They will definitely be friends forever.

EIGHT

KATELYN

Monday Night - Two Days After the Party

It feels like she is moving through mud, her body heavy with exhaustion, her mind clouded in fog as she keeps going back to the party, trying to remember exactly when it was that she lost her memory. It is a slippery thread that she keeps grabbing, only to lose hold of immediately.

She is sitting at the kitchen table, staring down at a container of pad thai, her stomach churning at the sweetish smell and the thought of the feel of the rice noodles in her mouth.

'Aren't you hungry?' asks Toby, dipping his chicken into satay sauce. 'It's what you always get.'

'I know.' She sighs. 'I'm just...' She sits back in her chair. She would love a drink but the doctor told her to avoid alcohol and there is no way she wants to trigger another event. 'Can you tell me again what happened?'

Toby stops eating and wipes his mouth with a white paper serviette. 'We were cleaning up after the party and you started repeating yourself and asking the same questions again and again and you seemed so confused and upset. We had no idea what happened.'

'But what were we discussing?' she asks because this is what she really wants to know. While she was lying on her bed, waiting for Toby to return with the takeaway food, she had googled transient global amnesia, wanting more than what the doctor has told her. She hadn't been having sex, obviously, so that ruled out the condition being caused by orgasm, which sounded incredibly weird. And she hadn't suddenly immersed herself in freezing water, which seemed to cause it for some people. She hadn't been doing strenuous exercise because all she was doing was cleaning up after a party. So that left stress or being emotionally upset by something, which she believes is what happened. It feels like the right explanation. She has no idea why that is but the feeling is a tiny nugget of certainty in her foggy brain.

'Just, you know, people at the party and... stuff, I guess.' The answer makes sense because Leah has been at every party she and Toby have had together, and before that at every party Katelyn had when she was still single; and after every party the best part of the whole thing had been the debrief with Leah, where they discussed who was dating who, who was getting married, who had a new job and who had a nose job. But there is something in the way Toby is trying to shrug off the discussion they were having that is making her question the truth.

'Why won't you discuss this?' she asks, pushing the container away from her and reaching for the Diet Coke Toby has poured for her, relishing the sharp, cold taste.

'I am discussing this, but there's no point in going over it. It won't help you remember. They told us you won't remember. And it completely freaked me out. It's like you were suddenly just gone and I thought...' He looks away from her. 'I thought it was permanent.' His voice is husky with emotion.

'I'm fine, I'm really fine,' she reassures him and he smiles.

'You are, of course you are.'

'Something must have happened, something to make my brain... lose everything. I can't remember the whole party,' she says. 'I can't even remember Leah arriving.'

Toby is a lawyer and if he doesn't want to talk about something he won't. He specialises in divorce law and he's very good at his job. He's represented some very famous people and no matter how hard she has tried to get juicy details out of him, she has failed. He never talks unless he wants to. And she can see that it's upsetting for him to discuss it, so she is wary of pushing.

'I just want to remember,' she says softly.

'Your episode could have begun during the party, or just before the party, but because it was loud and lots of people were talking and there were a lot of things going on, people around you were unaware that something was wrong,' the neurologist told her this morning.

'Look, I don't know what to tell you, Kate,' says Toby, opening his container of red curry and eating it like he's starving. 'My mum picked up Harper about two hours before Leah arrived and you seemed fine, relaxed even. You worked really hard to make the place look nice and you were tired, so maybe that was it. Maybe all the planning and stuff was just too much.' He stops eating and takes a sip of his beer, his gaze focused not on her but at the kitchen wall behind her.

'Toby,' she says, 'is there something you're not telling me? Something that happened that you're keeping from me? I know you're worried but I need to know what happened at the party or after the party because it may help me to get my memory back.'

The message from Aaron has been on repeat in her head the whole day. She's almost grateful that it keeps going around and around because it is evidence that she can remember something that she read hours ago.

I'm so, so sorry about everything that happened at the party and I'm here to talk. You know where to find me when you're ready.

What did he mean?

Toby shrugs and puts down his beer. 'Nothing happened. It was a party. People had fun. That's all there is to it. Listen,' he says, standing up and picking up his half-empty container of food, 'I may just go and answer some work emails. I've had the graduate working on some stuff and I think she's run into some trouble so I want to just check she hasn't sent out anything that could come back to bite me. Are you going to be okay?' He is so polite, so solicitous that he sounds like a different person, but maybe she's the one who's different. Or maybe he just wants to get away from her and her questions.

'Where are all the pictures?' she asks. 'I looked through my phone and I only have one of Leah and I just before the party started. Where are they all?'

Toby puts his fork and spoon in the dishwasher and his beer bottle in the recycling and then grabs himself another beer. 'Leah has them on her phone. She was in charge of taking photos but other people did too. You can contact them and ask but I don't know if you want to tell people what happened, or leave it. I guess you could just say that you're collecting photographs.' He says the words as he's walking out of the kitchen as though he doesn't want a reply from her and she sighs, not wanting to force him to stay with her when he has been watching over her all day.

'I'll ask her to come over and show me, maybe later tonight,' she says, turning in her chair to watch him.

Toby stops. 'Why tonight? Give it some more time. You need to rest. Why don't you go upstairs and have a bath, or something? I'll clean up the rest after I've finished my emails. I have to go in tomorrow but I'll try and make it home early. I've just got someone coming in that I can't reschedule. Mum will drop Harper off at school and then come here and sit with you.'

'Please tell her not to,' says Katelyn, the idea of being watched all day long making her feel claustrophobic. 'I'm fine and I just need some time alone, if that's okay.'

'I don't think—' begins Toby.

'Please,' she says again. 'Just a few hours and then I'll pick up Harper. I'm fine. I really am. I think we should talk more about the party.'

'There's nothing to talk about and I'm not having any discussions now. You look exhausted. Go and rest.'

Katelyn nods obligingly and turns around to stare down at her food again. She's not getting anything from him now and she is so tired. Toby leaves and Katelyn looks around the kitchen at the white marble benchtop and the grey cabinets that she and the decorator decided on when they were renovating the kitchen. She had driven to the Blue Mountains to buy the handles for the cabinets from a woman who made them in her backyard. If she closes her eyes, she can see the woman's house with its jumble of metal lying on large worn timber tables and her dogs barking behind a fence. She renovated the kitchen when she was pregnant with Harper and she can remember every detail of the project. Why can't she remember a stupid party?

Frustrated, she stands and thinks about cleaning up for only a moment, before leaving the mess for Toby like he said to do.

Upstairs in her bedroom she has a shower instead of a bath and gets into a pair of warm, comfortable pyjamas covered in cats – chosen for her by Harper last time they went shopping. 'Look at the cute kitties, Mum, and there's one in my size as well, can we get them please, please?' her daughter begged, her green eyes shining. Katelyn smiles at the memory every time she wears the pyjamas.

She turns out the light and gets into bed, lying still for only a minute before she turns on her lamp and stares up at the ceiling. Picking up her phone she scrolls through all the texts, wondering if she finally has the energy to reply to them but she doesn't. There are a few texts from Leah.

Heard you're home, text me whenever.

Hey Kate, hope you're okay, let me know if you need help with Harper tomorrow.

Hey Kate, give me a call when I can come over.

Inside her, a strange desire not to speak to Leah is almost a physical sensation. She has never not wanted to speak to Leah. Maybe she's just not ready to speak to anyone at all. She turns on her side to put her phone back on her bedside table and in doing so hits a small pink ring holder shaped like a tiny tree off the table, scattering the rings hanging off it onto the floor.

'Shit,' she curses and she gets off the bed and onto her hands and knees, picking up the rings. Two of them are her engagement ring – a band of white gold studded with diamonds and sapphires – and her wedding ring – a simple ring of white gold with a single diamond in the centre. Why would she have taken them off, since she usually only took them off as she got into bed? Maybe Toby took them from her in the hospital because she was being sent for tests – that makes sense. He came upstairs for a shower after they'd done some cleaning in the house, so perhaps he put them on the ring holder then. She has a sudden sensation of removing the rings herself. *Why would I have done that?*

The other two rings are more costume jewellery. One of them was a present from Harper after attending her first Mother's Day stall at preschool this year. All the children had been told to bring five dollars and they could choose a present for their mothers.

Harper had been bursting with excitement when she unwrapped the small ring box to find a silver ring with a red mushroom covered in silver dots.

'It's the prettiest ring ever,' said Harper and Katelyn had to agree, proudly wearing it out to brunch with Maureen and Ted.

The last ring is a Celtic band in silver that Leah gave her when they were teenagers. She had given Leah exactly the same thing for her birthday that year. They had seen the rings in a store one Saturday and both fallen in love with them. 'Let's get one for each of us and give them to each other on our birthdays,' Leah said. Katelyn had agreed to the expensive present, even though it took most of her savings. She places the band on the ring holder with the other two.

But she cannot find the mushroom ring and she leans down and looks under the bed, moving her hand along the plush cream carpet searching for it. She finds it quickly but as she's moving her hand away it touches something else, a box.

Katelyn pulls it out. It's a pink and white striped Victoria's Secret box, tied with a black ribbon. There is a small card attached. *I can imagine you in this*, it says, in neat printed letters done by computer.

Toby doesn't give her underwear. He thinks it's something she should buy for herself and they've been together for ten years now. Her desire to wear sexy underwear disappeared as she struggled with her body after she had Harper, the weight falling off as she dealt with the sleepless nights and lack of time to eat. He knows that about her and he wouldn't have bought this for her.

With trembling fingers, she opens the box and moves aside the tissue paper to find a cherry-red bra and matching thong. Not something she would ever wear.

More like something Leah would wear.

Lifting the bra, she touches the smooth silk of the thong. They would probably fit her but it's so completely not her style. The bra drops from her hands as though hot and her heart is loud in her ears as an image comes at her like a brick to her head.

Toby and Leah enclosed in a tight hug, her arms around his back and her head on his chest.

Katelyn drops the box on the floor and moves away as though it might bite. No. She didn't see that. She's making it up, it's some weird glitch, but the picture is seared in her mind. Toby is wearing the white shirt he was wearing at the hospital and Leah is in the white jeans and low-cut silver-coloured top she had bought specifically for the celebration. She's wearing those clothes in the phone picture Katelyn has of the two of them before the party. She shakes her head. Her brain is playing tricks on her and she's only 'remembering' because she's putting images together in a desperate attempt to figure out what happened.

Downstairs she hears the familiar sounds of Toby cleaning up the kitchen, meaning he will come upstairs soon.

Shoving everything back in the box and pushing the box far under the bed, Katelyn gets back into bed, her eyes overflowing as she switches off her bedside lamp. She wipes quickly at her face as she hears Toby coming up the stairs and opening the bedroom door softly. Turning on her side she fakes the deep breathing of sleep, her heart pounding in her ears until she hears the door close softly.

She lies still for five minutes, her ears straining for the sound of Toby going back downstairs, but instead she hears him go into Harper's room and close the door. Is he going to sleep in there? Why would he do that? They've never slept apart.

Katelyn closes her eyes as she breathes deeply in and out, trying to calm her racing heart. The fear that any moment now she will simply disappear again hovers in the back of her mind.

I am in my bed in my house. I got home from the hospital about five hours ago. It's Monday and Toby picked up Thai food for dinner.

Satisfied with these facts she feels her body begin to calm down when she remembers the box of underwear. Maybe that didn't happen?

Switching on her bedside lamp again, she climbs out of bed and reaches for the box underneath, bitterness filling her mouth when she feels the solid shape. Once again, she pulls it out and looks at the contents and then she shoves everything back in the box, wishing she could throw it in the garbage.

Is her husband cheating on her? Is he cheating on her with her best friend? She pushes the box far under the bed, standing up in a rush. She'll ask him right now. If he lies, she'll know.

At the door a wave of dizziness assaults her, her stomach churning. Darting for the bathroom, she empties her stomach. Sweat covers her body as she leans over her basin to rinse her mouth. She's in no position to do anything right now. Any energy she had for a confrontation drains away.

Toby and Leah are just friends. They have been 'just friends' since they broke up. Since they broke up just before Toby and Katelyn started dating. Just before.

'They're just friends,' Katelyn whispers.

Her head pounds as she climbs back into bed.

What was Aaron's text about? What did it mean and why is he sorry? Is it something to do with Toby and Leah, or something separate? Katelyn would like to turn off her brain, to just stop thinking, but she's terrified that everything will disappear again, that she will disappear again. But she knows she needs to sleep.

Mentally counting backwards from one hundred she wills her body into sleep, hoping that in the morning her life will be back to the way it was, but even as she drifts off she knows this is impossible, feels it's impossible, but she has no idea why.

NINE

LEAH

Her phone is clutched in her hand as she lies on her bed and stares up at the ceiling. She has applied for six jobs today, changing her résumé each time to fit the key performance indicators on the list of skills needed and trying hard to hit the right note of interested and yet not desperate every time. Running in the background of her mind has been the night of the party. Katelyn hasn't replied to her numerous texts and each time she sends one she really hopes she doesn't, which is a really strange feeling and one that she's not used to. If Katelyn hadn't lost her memory, they would never speak to each other again, Leah's sure of that, and she feels like she's now in some kind of weird limbo where they are still friends, but only one of them knows they shouldn't be. And she keeps thinking about Toby and Harper.

Harper is always delighted to see Leah, running and jumping into her arms and making Leah feel welcome whenever she arrives. Leah knows that if she had the gift of a bubbly gorgeous three-year-old like Harper she would never want to leave her alone even for a minute and she has never been able to understand Katelyn's constant need for space from the child, never been able to understand Katelyn's constant complaints about being woken early and never having enough time for herself.

On Saturday night, as she always did, Leah had a terrible urge to shake her best friend and shout, 'You have no idea how grateful you should be, no idea at all.'

Katelyn loved her daughter with a passion and Leah knew that. Every mother had moments of feeling frustrated and trapped and Leah knew that as well, but she couldn't help getting angry with Katelyn when she complained. Katelyn had nothing to complain about.

In her hand her phone clicks with an incoming text and Leah sighs when she sees it's from Toby.

I've been thinking about this and I think we have to just never talk about what happened.

'Of course,' spits Leah and then she texts back.

Katelyn should know the truth. She should know what happened and then be able to decide how things go from here.

Staring at her phone she waits for his answer for nearly two minutes, her anger mounting with each passing second.

I don't want to say anything to her. I just want my life back. She seems to have forgotten everything. It's like it never happened at all and I want to keep it this way. I know this is not what we discussed, but I feel like I have a second chance with her and we're a family. I need to think about Harper. I'm sorry, Leah, really sorry. But please understand – there's a child to consider. I know what happens to kids when marriages break up. Please let's just forget it.

Leah doesn't reply, furiously bursting into hot angry tears. This is not how it was supposed to end, not at all, and there's no way she's going to just forget it, no way at all.

And Katelyn shouldn't be allowed to just move on from what she did, while Leah has to suffer and remember. Toby shouldn't be allowed to pretend he and Leah were never closely aligned in what they wanted.

A part of Leah still suspects that Katelyn has orchestrated the whole thing to get away with everything.

And what about what you did, she hears as though she has actually spoken aloud, but she bats the words away. She did what she had to do, what she needed to do.

Sighing, she gets out of bed and goes to her kitchen for something to drink, pouring some milk into a pan to heat up for cocoa and grabbing a biscuit. She can feel she's gaining weight from all the snacking she is doing as she looks for a job.

Her kitchen is small and filled with white cabinets and finished with a plain black granite countertop. It looks like every rental unit ever and she hates it.

'How did this become my life?' she asks the white tiled walls.

Katelyn is home in bed with her husband by her side and she is here alone when she should be with a person who loves her.

She thinks about Toby, about the way he rubs his eyes under his glasses when he's tired, and the way he gestures with his hands when he speaks. He had worn the shirt she chose for him to the party and he had looked as good as she thought he would.

In her bedroom her phone pings with a text and she debates

with herself about ignoring it, but she's never ignored a text in her life.

Hey, hi, it was so great to catch-up at the party. Just wanted to invite you to my birthday lunch next week. Us pregnant ladies have to stick together. I don't know if you're still feeling nauseous but we're having it at that little vegetarian place on Strand Street. Let me know if you can come. And sorry again about the drink Rob got you. He didn't know you were on virgin margaritas but at least you worked it out after the first sip – although I'm sure you nearly finished it but that must be my pregnancy brain (ha ha). Thanks for trusting me with your big secret.

Abigail has finished her text with an annoying string of baby and smiling emojis. She can feel Abigail's judgement at Leah's consumption of alcohol through the phone.

Leah stares down at Abigail's message, cursing her stupidity. She should never have said anything and now she has no idea how she's going to get out of this.

In her kitchen she pours the cocoa into a mug and thinks about texting Katelyn again. Whenever something huge has happened in her life, the first person she has told has been Katelyn, most of the time before she's even told her parents. But now the huge thing that has happened is looming over everything and probably means the end of their friendship and she has no idea where she goes from here.

She drinks her cocoa in bed, scrolling through Instagram until she has seen a million babies and a million happy families and her eyes are burning, everything she will never have choking her as she tries to swallow the overly sweet cocoa. She had fantasised about the pregnancy photo shoot before she even had a husband and she knew how it would look, how it was supposed to look. Leah, glowing with a beautiful man by her side, his hand resting gently on her rounded bump. Leah alone and miserable was not anything she had ever planned.

Katelyn should be the one who can't sleep and Leah lets the hot feeling of hate she has for her old friend travel up from her toes, until she grabs a pillow and screams into it until her throat hurts.

This is not going to be how things end – not at all.

She sleeps soundly after that.

TEN

Leah picks up some cups that have been dropped on the carpet and puts them into a garbage bin. People became such animals at a party. Katelyn is moving between groups of people, but even though she is supposed to be telling them to eat from the buffet table she seems to be distracted by every conversation going on with each group of people. Instead, it is Toby who is asking people to get food and not leave them with 'too many leftovers'.

Leah leans down to pick up an empty plastic plate and sees a wrapped box sitting next to the wall, behind a timber side table. It's obviously a birthday gift for Katelyn that has not made it into the study with all the other birthday gifts.

She picks up the box, admiring the lush pink ribbon around the striped paper, and moves towards the study to put it with the others.

She stops near the door, hearing voices inside, and waits because she immediately recognises Aaron's low rumble.

Sidling closer to the slightly open door so she can hear over

Beyoncé singing about fantasies being fulfilled, she bends her head, strains, desperate to know what he's saying and who he's talking to in private. It must be a woman.

'You look really beautiful tonight,' Aaron says and Katelyn giggles. Leah knows it is Katelyn's giggle because she's been listening to that giggle since she was six years old.

'And you're so handsome,' she replies.

Leah feels her stomach turn. It's not that she and Katelyn never discussed how good-looking Aaron is, it's that this feels like a betrayal. Why is her friend being nice to this man after everything he did to Leah?

Disgusted, she moves away, tucking the present under her arm and taking her phone out and snapping pictures of everyone enjoying themselves. At least with her phone in her hand she can move from group to group without having to have the divorce conversation.

Leah makes her way back into the kitchen where she shoves the gift behind the coffee machine.

'Hey, Leah, how are you?' she hears as she turns to find Jason Elland in the kitchen.

'So good.' She grins. Jason has lost most of his hair and developed a beer belly but at least he's a friendly face.

'Great.' He smiles. 'You look amazing.'

'Thank you.' She grins back.

'My wife is like a million months pregnant. I can't even remember the last time she wore jeans,' he muses.

Leah is instantly done with the conversation. 'Oh well, she'll be back in those jeans soon. Congratulations on the baby.' She moves away even before he's managed to get the words, 'Thank you,' out.

The house heaves with people, crowded into every corner of the living room, the air filled with mingling smells of perfume, melted cheese and the sharp whiff of alcohol.

Leah longs for quiet. Every song on the playlist makes her

feel older by the minute, but Katelyn loves the songs from their teenage years.

She wishes she could climb under a table with a bowl of corn chips and some salsa and just stay there until the party is over. That way she could avoid seeing Aaron who is now holding court with some of the men, lecturing security and football or basketball, some sport. But she's promised to take photographs, to help keep the buffet table full, to perform best friend duties.

She fills a glass with red wine, overfills it and when she lifts it to her lips, some of it spills on her tight silver top, the smell irritating her so she puts the wine down and returns to the alcoholic slushie machine. One more won't matter.

Everyone she sees wants to discuss her divorce so she needs all the help she can get to deal with the raised eyebrows and sympathetic looks. There is a queue for the raspberry-flavoured ice concoction and she has no desire to wait. She'll gather a few smug smiles of sympathy and return in a few minutes.

Throwing her shoulders back she moves away from the drinks table towards a group of old school friends, her phone up, ready to snap photos.

'Leah,' her friend Abigail screeches as she walks past her. 'Oh my God, I haven't seen you for absolute ages. How are you? What have you been up to?' Abigail has curly red hair and pale-green eyes and she was in the same year at school as Katelyn and Leah. At school she was teased for her face full of freckles but she was still beautiful. She had actually been closer to Leah than she was to Katelyn. But that changed when they both got married in the same year and then both had children at the same time. Now Abigail's little boy, Harry – who shares her red hair and green eyes – goes to preschool with Harper and Katelyn and Abigail speak nearly every day. Leah longs for another drink. She should have just waited in the queue.

'Oh, you know,' Leah says, raising her voice so she can be

heard over the music, 'the usual.' She had made a decision before the party to keep her answers to everything as vague as possible and just hope that no one had heard about her spectacular failure at work, but even as she made the decision she understood that it would be an almost impossible thing. Somebody would know someone who would have heard via the grapevine that Leah had been fired for her screw-up. Abigail's husband Rob is standing next to her. He's always reminded Leah of a plastic Ken doll with his perfect flat brown hair and square jaw. He looks around the room, searching for someone more interesting to talk to. 'Can I get you ladies a drink?' he asks.

'Sure,' answers Leah. 'I'll have another cocktail from the slushie machine.'

'Great and I'll get you some mineral water, darling,' he says, moving off and away from them.

'The cocktails are delicious,' says Leah and Abigail laughs.

'Not for me,' she says and then she steps right up to Leah. 'We're pregnant. Don't say anything. I haven't told many people.' She gives Leah a Cheshire cat grin.

'Congratulations,' says Leah, her stomach heavy. Abigail is not keeping her pregnancy a secret. She has just shouted the news to Leah who she sees every few months at the most and Leah is willing to bet that right now a scheduled post along with a cute picture of a sonogram is going up on Instagram. Soon there will be a fluttering of interested women around Abigail asking how far along she is, if she knows the sex of the child, how she's feeling, how her son is feeling about becoming a big brother... and on and on. Leah has heard a thousand of the same conversations.

'What about you?' asks Abigail. 'Any plans for a baby? I know people are waiting longer and longer but they do say that our fertility falls off a cliff after thirty-five, don't they?' Another Cheshire cat grin. Abigail knows she's divorced.

Rob returns with the drinks and Leah takes hers gratefully. 'How's work?' he asks her and she nods. 'Good,' she says, but then she meets his gaze and realises that he knows. Of course he does. Rob works in marketing for a sneaker brand.

A streak of visceral hatred for the smug couple in front of her races through Leah and she takes a large sip of her drink and says, 'Oh, sorry... I promised Katelyn I'd help with...' and she turns and walks away.

Katelyn is talking to another old school friend, a drink of something pink in her hand. 'Hey, what are you drinking?' Leah asks coming to stand next to her and Katelyn turns to look at her and then blinks. 'Hey, Leah... my best friend, Leah,' she says.

'Wow, you're really drunk,' laughs Leah.

'No, I'm... I'm drunk,' laughs Katelyn. 'You look so sexy.'

'You told me that already, maybe you should have some food.'

'Leah, Leah, Leah, my best friend, Leah,' sings Katelyn loudly. 'I have so much to tell you.'

'You're being weird,' says Leah, finding Katelyn annoying, finding the whole party more than a little annoying. She would leave now if she could but Katelyn would never forgive her. Katelyn loves the party debrief.

'What do you have to tell me?' Leah asks as the other woman moves off.

'I don't know,' says Katelyn. 'What do I have to tell you?'

'You should stop drinking now,' says Leah, turning away from her friend.

'You should stop drinking,' repeats Katelyn and then she laughs.

Leah doesn't want to be here anymore.

Someone runs, actually runs, past her holding a long line of silver tinsel.

'I need the bathroom,' she says to Katelyn who nods and

takes a sip of her drink and then wrinkles her nose like it disgusts her. 'I need some more chips,' she says.

Leah turns away from her friend, and making sure that no one is watching, she goes up the stairs to Katelyn's bedroom to use the en-suite bathroom, to get some space, to be alone.

It is comforting to close Katelyn's bedroom door behind her, to block out the music and overly loud laughter from everyone proving how much of a good time they are having.

Leah ducks into the bathroom and finds some lip balm, smooths it across her lips as she studies herself in the mirror. The white jeans and silver top work well together, showing off the body she works so hard for.

Katelyn's perfume stands on the marble countertop and Leah picks it up, sprays some on her skin and sniffs. It smells different on her to how it does on Katelyn, too sweet.

Opening each drawer of the vanity cabinet, she runs her hands along Katelyn's things and touches the brush Toby uses and the face cream Katelyn bought for him.

She opens the bottom drawer and stops, crouches down, takes a closer look. She didn't know Katelyn still had old pregnancy tests.

Her stomach roils and she pulls down her pants and underwear, sits on the toilet, holding a pregnancy test in her hand. *Imagine.*

Five minutes later she is downstairs, the pregnancy test stowed in her bag.

She should have just stayed downstairs, carried on drinking.

ELEVEN

KATELYN AND LEAH – TWENTY-SIX YEARS OLD

'You look stunning,' breathes Leah as she watches Katelyn twirl in the mirror, the white lace dress with an underlay of pale pink floating around her.

'I love this dress so much,' says Katelyn.

'I knew as soon as you put it on it was the one for you,' agrees Leah.

She does look stunning with her chestnut hair half up and down, curls trailing down her back, and her green eyes shadowed in smoky grey. It's the most beautiful Leah has ever seen her friend look, but perhaps that has more to do with how happy she is.

'I can't believe I'm actually getting married,' says Katelyn.

'Me neither,' says Leah. 'I can't actually imagine ever doing it myself.'

The great commitment of marriage seems to Leah to be something for her future self. Right now, all she wants to do is work hard and enjoy the weekends. She had never expected to get into university but when she had, she had decided on a business and communications degree. And now she has what she can only think of as her dream job. The online make-up company, We Adore You, is still small, still finding its way in the market but Leah loves everything about it. It's not her company but she's been there since it was just three people. Her job was answering phones at first, but now she is leading the push for marketing. She's done everything. Her bathroom cabinet is filled with samples from every make-up company in the world and she spends hours on the phone each night, calling overseas and promoting their website. Katelyn has not been as lucky with work and Leah thinks her desire to marry may have something to do with that. Working for an online homewares company on the back end of their website has little to do with Katelyn's art history degree.

'Are you ready for the veil?' Leah asks and Katelyn nods, so Leah picks up the wisp of netting from the hotel bed and uses the hair comb to attach it to Katelyn's head. 'Perfect,' she says as she stares at the two of them in the mirror. Leah is wearing a sheath dress in matching pale pink and her hair is pulled back into a high ponytail, her blue eyes shadowed to match Katelyn's.

There is a light knock at the door and Katelyn calls, 'Come in.'

Leah's father Isaac stands at the door in a black tux with a crisp white shirt. 'Don't you look a picture, Katelyn,' he says, 'and aren't you beautiful, darling,' he murmurs to Leah.

'Thank you,' says Katelyn and Leah smiles. 'I'll just be out here when you're ready. The guests are all seated and the celebrant is ready to begin.'

'And Toby?' asks Katelyn, her voice raised with some panic, making Leah laugh.

'Of course he's there,' she says and her father nods and closes the door quietly.

'Ready?' asks Leah.

'Just, um... wait,' says Katelyn. 'I need you to tell me one more time that you're okay with your dad walking me down the aisle and that you're not angry about Toby even a little bit.'

'I've already said that I'm fine with both a thousand times, Kate. Why won't you believe me?'

Katelyn shakes her head and then blinks, as though holding back tears. 'He's your dad and Toby was yours first,' she says.

'First of all, my dad loves you, you know that, both my parents do. And second of all, I broke up with Toby, remember? We were too similar.' Leah means the words as she says them, but sometimes she wonders if she is really okay with it. Every time she sees them together, she reminds herself that Toby belongs with Katelyn and that she cannot change the past. The two of them just click and it seems that in every situation, they only have eyes for each other. They should be married and together forever.

'I know.' Katelyn smiles. 'You both like the kitchen cleaned within an inch of its life and you both love caramel and hate chocolate and you both stay up too late but fall asleep instantly.'

'And so many other things. I like him, he's a good guy, but we only dated for a couple of months.' The words almost get stuck, almost.

'I know but I'm still... I wish I'd met him on my own.' Katelyn has repeated this sentiment over and again for the six months that she and Toby have been dating because it's something that will never stop bothering her. She and Leah met Toby at the same time when he was brought home by Leah's father Isaac. 'They've told us we have to be nice to the graduate lawyers and invite them home for dinner so they can see how wonderful life can be if they keep working very hard all hours of the day,' Isaac told Leah who explained it to Katelyn. 'There are two of them coming but Mum and I need backup, so the two of you come over as well and the young people can talk.'

The night of the dinner, Katelyn was running late and so

told Leah she would meet her at her mother's house. When she walked into the dining room and saw Toby, her heart jumped in her chest in a way that she had not imagined possible. The lanky young man with large brown eyes was sitting next to Leah, talking animatedly about something, his hands moving all the time.

'Kate,' said Leah when she saw her. 'Come and meet Toby. He's just moved here from Melbourne with his family and he knows absolutely no one except boring lawyers so I'm taking him out tomorrow night.'

Katelyn remembers smiling obligingly and then forcing herself to make polite conversation, even as she wanted to tell Leah to stay away from Toby. She had not felt that way about a man since she'd been a sixteen-year-old girl and had hankered after Jason Elland. The other graduate lawyer was a woman who seemed so uncomfortable that Katelyn couldn't help but feel sorry for her. She concentrated on her over dinner, trying to get her to reply with more than just one word, quizzing her about her family and what kind of law she wanted to practise eventually. On the way home, Leah had gushed about how cute Toby was, how intelligent, how funny, how tall, how everything and Katelyn had put him firmly out of her mind. Men like Toby and Jason were not for her. They were for the graceful, beautiful Leahs of the world. Katelyn was pretty, petite and shy. She blended in rather than stood out, but everyone's eyes turned to Leah as soon as she walked into a room.

Leah and Toby saw each other a few times over the following weeks. When Toby arrived at the apartment Katelyn and Leah shared, Leah was usually running late, believing that men benefitted from waiting for her, and Katelyn and Toby would spend time together, just chatting. Each time Leah and Toby left for their date, Katelyn would feel heavy with disappointment. Toby loved art and history just like she did but he and Leah were similar in so many ways, loving the same food and having the same taste in books and movies.

When Leah told her that she and Toby were not really suited, Katelyn didn't know how to react. 'Why?' she asked.

'It's like dating myself really. We both like exactly the same things and we almost think the same way about everything. It's boring. He's lovely but... I don't know, not really exciting, I guess,' she said, wrinkling her nose. It was a Saturday night, usually a night Leah was out with Toby or whoever she was dating and a night when Katelyn mostly stayed home and watched romantic movies alone. She struggled with meeting men, finding herself rendered silent in bars when other young women were happy to chat about anything. She had been surprised when Leah told her she would be home but excited to spend the night with her, sharing the pizza they ordered and catching up. When Leah told her she and Toby were over, Katelyn felt her heart lift.

'When did you decide that?'

'I told him on the phone a couple of hours ago. He took it pretty well but I just felt like I didn't want to go out with him. I would rather spend the night on the sofa with my bestie so that made me realise that I didn't really like him all that much.'

They were sitting next to each other on the plush green-velvet sofa they had bought together when they moved into the rental unit, watching *Twilight* on DVD, but the moment Leah said that she and Toby were over, Katelyn stopped hearing anything the actors were saying.

'He's such a nice guy,' Katelyn said carefully.

'Yeah, but not for me. You should date him,' she said suddenly, seemingly enchanted with the idea. 'I mean it's not like he and I were ever serious and he likes you. I can tell he does. You date him.'

Leah probably expected Katelyn to refuse, to say that she had no interest in Toby, but she somehow couldn't say that. 'You wouldn't mind?' she asked, struggling to keep her excitement out of her voice.

'Nah,' said Leah and they spent the rest of the evening discussing Robert Pattinson and sharing a bottle of wine and some popcorn.

Katelyn waited three days before she called Toby with her heart in her mouth and asked him for coffee.

Leah hadn't minded. She always said that she was happy for both of them but Katelyn needed to hear Leah tell her that again, especially on her wedding day.

'I promise, I am so, so happy for you both,' says Leah, her smile wide.

'Okay,' breathes Katelyn.

She opens the door and together with Isaac, the two girls walk down the maroon carpeted stairs of the boutique hotel in the Blue Mountains where Toby and Katelyn have chosen to marry. It's an old hotel, a little shabby but still holding the beauty of its past with ceiling roses and heavy velvet curtains everywhere. Even the hotel would not have been affordable as a wedding venue if Toby's parents hadn't offered to pay.

'It's mostly my family anyway,' Toby said gently when she tried to refuse the offer, and Katelyn had to admit that was the truth.

Her mother had passed away when she and Leah were on a trip overseas after school. When they left, her mother had been in a sober phase, even working as a waitress at a local café.

Katelyn and Leah had been backpacking around Europe for six weeks together before starting university and a neighbour had called Katelyn to let her know that there were parcels piling up outside their apartment. When Katelyn couldn't get hold of her mother, Leah asked her father to go over and the building manager let him in. 'I think it was a heart attack,' Isaac wrote in an email the girls read together in an internet café in Rome.

'We should go home early,' said Leah.

'No... we have three days left, we can finish our trip,' said Katelyn. She felt numb, filled with despair, and also there was some small amount of relief. She had been waiting for this for so long. Every morning of her childhood she had woken and if she couldn't hear her mother moving around the apartment, she had gone to check if she was breathing, holding a finger under her mother's nose and waiting for the feel of air. She would never have to check again.

Her mother had hugged her before she left and promised to remain sober, but even though Katelyn had said, 'You will, I know you will,' she hadn't believed it. She knew that her mother would start drinking again, had been waiting for it for months, and now she didn't have to wait anymore. When they got home, Katelyn understood that her mother had started drinking again almost as soon as she left on her trip. She had lost her job four weeks before she died and the neglected apartment was filled with empty bottles, random strange parcels from Amazon were filled with pet toys and kitchen gadgets for a woman who didn't have a pet and rarely cooked. At her mother's funeral she hadn't even been able to cry, having used up all her tears every time her mother started drinking again.

She's an only child and her father had never been in the picture and although she knows that her mother has relatives in South Australia, Katelyn had never met any of them, not even her grandmother. 'She kicked me out when she found out I was pregnant, another thing you ruined,' Katelyn's mother told her once after a heavy drinking session. Leah and her family were the only real family Katelyn had. She had invited some of her work colleagues and old friends from school but Toby's large family took up most of the guest list. His sister had come from London for the wedding, bringing her two adorable sons with her, and Katelyn had quickly bonded with Quinn over Toby's quirks.

Katelyn takes a deep breath as they stand at the double

doors that close off the reception area. She closes her eyes briefly and thanks God for her luck, for the wonderful luck that has led her to Toby and his family because now she has a huge family too, filled with love and joy.

As Isaac and the girls enter the room where the wedding guests are seated, Leah looks over at Toby as he runs a finger around his collar, pulling it away from his throat and then rubs his eyes under his glasses as though unable to believe how beautiful Katelyn looks.

Leah walks slowly up the aisle, noticing as people smile at her, as men gaze at her, but she can see that Toby only has eyes for his bride. She dismisses a burning feeling in her stomach. She's not jealous of Katelyn, not at all. If she ever wanted Toby, she knows that she could get him back. She smiles wider, pushing the unkind thought out of her head.

Not that she would do that, of course. Katelyn is her best friend. They have been best friends forever and there is no way she would do that to her. She is happy that Katelyn finally has a husband and a new family because Toby's parents seem to love her. Now Katelyn will be with her husband instead of Leah at Christmas and they will visit his parents instead of celebrating at Leah's house, and Leah is fine with that. One day she will find her Prince Charming and she will have everything Katelyn has now, every single thing.

TWELVE

KATELYN

Tuesday – Three Days After the Party

When she wakes in the morning, Toby is already gone. She has slept fitfully, almost afraid to be asleep in case her memory disappeared somewhere in the night hours, stealing away everything. She had gotten up twice during the night to go to the bathroom and make sure that she remembered the day and time and where she was, whispering the words to the mirror as she studied her face. 'It's Tuesday, 2 a.m., I'm home in my bathroom. I was in the hospital because I lost my memory but I'm fine now. I'm fine now.'

Stretching across the bed as sunlight creeps around the edges of the curtains, she goes through what she knows for sure. It's Tuesday and Toby has gone to work because he has a client he can't reschedule. Harper is being dropped at preschool by Maureen. Turning on her side she picks up her phone and confirms the date and then reads a text from Maureen.

Harper was an absolute angel, slept through the night and has had Grandpa's special banana pancakes for breakfast. I've

*dropped her off and let them know you'll be picking her up.
Call me when you're feeling up to it. I'm happy to come
over xxx*

*I'm absolutely fine, thanks so much for having her. You're the
best grandmother ever! xxx*

There is also a text from Leah from early this morning,
asking if she should come over. Katelyn cannot see Leah, cannot
even look at her, but she also doesn't want to say anything to her
in case she is wrong about the image of her and Toby together
and wrong about what it means.

*Thanks, Toby is going in today but I'm fine. I know you have
work so please don't worry. Maureen is around if I need her x,*
she replies and then she looks around her bedroom where she
carefully chose the paint colour of cream with a hint of chocolate to warm the walls and matched the linen and carpet. This is
her safe space, her beautiful safe space, but it feels wrong today
as the box under the bed looms large in her mind.

Everything in the bedroom looks the same as it did yesterday. She will have to pick up Harper from preschool just like
she did last Tuesday and the Tuesday before that, as she has
done for months. Her memory has not disappeared. Everything
is the same and yet, everything is completely different.

In the light of a new day, the idea that Toby is cheating with
Leah seems preposterous, evidence of her mind not working
properly. But then who is the underwear for? Another woman?

The text from Aaron must be about something else. Maybe
Toby has found out about her and Aaron, but then why
wouldn't he have said when she asked about the party? Why
not just tell her he knows?

The room is warm and she can hear the soft hum of the
reverse cycle air conditioner, heating up the space. She is
suddenly oppressed by the stuffy air and throws off her caramel-

coloured duvet, leaping to her feet and going to switch off the heater. She jumps into the shower, letting the pounding water soothe her, and dresses in jeans and a jumper.

Downstairs the kitchen is clean and she opens the pantry, trying to figure out what to have for breakfast even though it's nearly 11 a.m. and closer to lunch.

Everything in the pantry is neatly lined up in perfect rows courtesy of Toby. Leah's pantry, or at least the cupboard in her small apartment she uses for a pantry, looks exactly the same. Katelyn has been nagging her about buying a place but Leah keeps telling her she's too busy to look for something at the moment. 'I'm fine in the rental,' she says.

It's an ongoing joke between the three of them that Katelyn chose a man to marry who is similar in personality to her best friend.

Leah met Toby first. Leah dated Toby first.

Ten years ago, Leah was already working for the cosmetics company where she is now the head of marketing and Katelyn was just starting her job with a new online company. Katelyn has only good memories from the few years she and Leah shared an apartment. For Katelyn it felt like the first time she had a real home where she was in complete control.

She and Leah shared dinner most nights, debriefing each other on their days, unless one of them had a date. They were both single, both looking for love but not desperately. Their apartment was located in a funky suburb near the city and they lived above a coffee shop that turned into a wine bar at night. They never minded the noise or the crowds. If neither of them had a date, they scrolled through the new Tinder app together, giggling as they read men's bios and trying to find the courage to swipe right. Leah was always game; Katelyn never was – so she spent a fair amount of time alone. And then they met Toby and Katelyn was sixteen all over again, until Leah and Toby broke up and Leah gave her permission to start dating Toby.

'I've been thinking of calling you for days,' was the first thing he said to her when she called him, and she had giggled.

'I needed to ask Leah if she was okay with me talking to you. Are you okay? Break-ups are hard.'

'I'm fine. I think we both felt the same way really. But I wouldn't want to never talk to you two again. She's a good friend. Do you want to get coffee with me sometime?'

'That's just what I was going to ask you,' she exclaimed. She knew she and Toby were going to get married after their first coffee date. But Leah took a lot longer to find her soulmate and it turned out he wasn't her soulmate at all. *Why are you even still speaking to him then? Why have you been spending time with him?* Katelyn dismisses the thought – she hasn't done anything wrong. Not yet.

Leah had been single for a long time, standing on the sidelines watching Katelyn get engaged and married and buy a house with Toby. When Leah met Aaron, an ex-army officer who owned a small security company, it seemed to be a perfect match.

'I knew Tinder would come through for me one day,' Leah had said after her first date with Aaron. There was no denying how attractive he was with his wide shoulders and square jaw. He wore his hair short and had piercing blue eyes and a deep laugh.

Katelyn settles on a bowl of muesli and pours in the milk, slumping onto a kitchen chair and putting her phone on the table. Everything is clean and tidy, as though the party never happened at all, which she supposes is the truth. For her, her memory stops... she has no idea when it stops. It feels like she remembers taking a selfie with Leah before the party but now she's not sure. She's not sure of anything.

Katelyn looks at the message from Aaron on her phone again and wonders what he meant. Does he know about Leah and Toby? Would she have seen them together and gone to tell him? He and Toby are good friends so maybe Toby has told him about another woman, but then why would Aaron tell her? Isn't there some sort of man code that prevents that?

Leah is hurting from her divorce and is worried that she won't find someone to have a child with and maybe she is questioning her decision to end things with Toby and maybe...

She spoons some of the muesli into her mouth, chewing mechanically.

Toby wouldn't cheat on her even if Leah threw herself at him. He's a good man and Leah is her best friend. They wouldn't betray her. Would they? And maybe the underwear is for her, a present from Toby to add a little spice to their lives. Maybe he wanted to give her something different this year, even though she told him not to bother with a gift because the party was her present. They have settled very comfortably into nights on the sofa watching Netflix. Perhaps Toby is hoping to change that. Katelyn doesn't love the idea of him buying her underwear but it makes sense. Toby just wants them to try something new. There is some relief in this thought but also some sadness. Toby wants more from their physical relationship. She does too but by the time Harper is asleep, all she wants is some space. Toby is obviously trying to change things.

She and Toby are happy, aren't they? Things were hard when Harper was little and even now, life as a stay-at-home mother is not what she thought it would be. Something that she never considered as she fought to have a child was the mind-numbing monotony of taking care of one. And she's terrified of repeating what happened when Harper was born, so she's told Toby that she doesn't want another child.

'One is enough for me,' she said, when he started talking about it last year. He picked the worst possible time to bring up the subject. They'd just had sex without Harper interrupting with calls for water or news of a bad dream and she was relaxed and drifting off into sleep when he said, 'Maybe you should go off the pill. It's better if siblings don't have such a large age gap.'

'No, I don't want to do that,' she said, her heart racing as she sat up in bed. 'One is enough for me. I don't want another child.'

Toby had stared at her for a few minutes and she had been able to see him digesting the information and she could also see him gritting his teeth slightly, a sure sign that he was angry and controlling it.

'We always discussed having two or three kids and one is not enough for me. And what about Harper? It's not fair to her to be an only child.'

'I was an only child—' began Katelyn.

'And you were lonely and sad and struggled to deal with your mother,' said Toby interrupting her.

'Are you saying I'm like my mother?' Katelyn snapped.

'Oh no, I'm not letting you turn this on me,' he said, getting out of bed and grabbing a T-shirt and pyjama pants. 'You're nothing like your mother and that's why I want another child with you. You don't get to just make this decision for both of us. We're a family.'

'And I'm the one who has to carry a child and give birth. I'm the one who has to take care of a baby while you swan off back to work in your nice suit and have lunch in a restaurant, while I'm up to my elbows in laundry and walking around like a zombie on no sleep.' The words had been backed by more anger than she knew she had and even as she finished speaking, she wished she had spoken slowly, considered what she wanted to say. She sounded irrational.

Toby had dropped the conversation but she knows he still desperately wants another child. She feels more incapable than ever of being a mother to two children now.

She sighs. She just wants to know what happened at the party. Everything will be clear once she knows that.

Picking up her phone she texts Aaron.

We need to speak.

Once the text is sent, she feels better.

Good idea, is his immediate response, *There's a lot to discuss. We need to meet somewhere we can talk.*

Katelyn stands up from her kitchen chair, suddenly restless and worried. She wishes he had just told her what he wanted to say, but perhaps it's better to speak to him in person. At least then she can look at him and judge whether he is telling her the truth or not.

Okay, she replies and then after thinking for a minute she sends him the name of a café she goes to and a time to meet.

I'll be there.

She assumed that he would tell her he was too busy to meet her today, but he hasn't done that and that makes Katelyn fearful that what happened was really awful.

She empties the remains of her cereal into the garbage. She can eat at the café. Right now, she needs to get ready.

Aaron will tell her the truth about the party. Someone has to tell her the truth.

A truth she hasn't revealed to Toby is that in the last three months she and Aaron have been speaking a lot more, spending time together.

Toby doesn't know about the plans she has been making with Aaron.

Maybe that's what this is about. Maybe Toby found out on the night of the party and he is not ready to confront Katelyn with it yet.

Maybe that's what he's hiding.

In the warm room, Katelyn shivers. Would Aaron have said

something to Toby? Surely not, they had an agreement. Katelyn wants to know this with certainty but nothing is certain, nothing can be trusted because she's not sure she can trust herself. That's the worst part of what happened. She's no longer sure she can trust herself.

THIRTEEN

LEAH

Tuesday – Three Days After the Party

When she opens her eyes, there is a moment between being fully awake and still drifting in her dreams and then the complete mess her life has become hits her with the force of a slap to the cheek and she raises her hands to cover her face, groaning aloud. She sent Katelyn a text this morning, asking if she wanted her to come over, and then she just stayed in bed and went back to sleep.

It's after 11 a.m. but there's no reason for her to get out of bed, so she grabs her phone and checks through the emails she has received. Her heart lifts a little when she sees three replies to jobs she has applied for.

She opens the first one, reads the top line. *Thank you for your application for the position of marketing manager with KRPC, unfortunately...* She stops reading when she sees that word and deletes the email immediately as though it may taint the others in her inbox.

But the other emails are tainted anyway with two more rejections. At some point she is either going to have to go to her parents for money, or go to the government for help – both options feel hideously humiliating and she cannot imagine which one of those would be worse.

Getting out of bed, she heads for the kitchen and a cup of coffee. Her kitchen is pristine because last night, lacking something to do, she cleaned and organised all her small cabinets. Usually, a tidy kitchen gives her some comfort but today she would like to take every cup, glass and plate out and smash them on the floor, shattering everything into small pieces. The expensive clay coffee cups and beautiful decorative crockery she got for her wedding don't belong in this place. Leah doesn't belong in this place.

With her coffee in her hand, she goes to the living room where she curls up on the sofa under a soft grey blanket. Katelyn has replied to her message telling her she doesn't need her, which stings. Katelyn has always needed Leah and even though Leah has no real desire to see her, she wants to feel needed. Perhaps she and Katelyn will never speak again, certainly not if Katelyn's memory returns.

On the way to the hospital Leah had simply put everything that happened at the party out of her mind, worried about Katelyn even as she questioned if she was actually pretending she couldn't remember things or not.

Opening her phone, she sips her coffee and scrolls through all the pictures she took at the party, starting with the selfie of her and Katelyn at the beginning. They had both used their phones at the same time so Katelyn has the same picture. If she puts these pictures up on Instagram everyone there will like and comment about how much fun they had because it had been fun, until it wasn't.

There are pictures of Katelyn with nearly all of the guests, in group shots or just with one person. In all of them Katelyn is smiling but now that she's looking through them, Leah can see that there is something off about her. Katelyn is smiling but looking closely, she sometimes appears confused, as though she has no idea why she is smiling and, in a couple, she seems to be looking at the person she is standing with as though she doesn't recognise them. Or maybe Leah is just seeing things, now that she knows what happened.

Leah remembers Katelyn asking her four times where she got her chunky white wedge heels from. Leah thought she was drunk, really drunk. Everything that she said and did on the night of the party could be attributed to the effects of alcohol.

She stops scrolling when she comes to a picture of Katelyn and Aaron together, standing close to each other but looking fairly awkward. Aaron hadn't exactly dressed for a party, wearing exactly the same thing he usually wore, tight black jeans and a black T-shirt that stretched across his broad shoulders. Leah had taken the picture reluctantly. She had been trying to avoid Aaron all night after finding the courage to greet him, only to have him turn away from her instantly to talk to someone else; but he came up to Katelyn just after Leah had taken a picture of her and Toby and said, 'I want a picture with the birthday girl.' Toby had obligingly stepped aside and Aaron had wrapped his arm around Katelyn's shoulders, his size making her seem even more petite than she was. 'Hi, Aaron,' Katelyn said, although she had obviously spoken to him when he arrived and had a weird conversation with him in the study. Leah had wanted to simply walk away from her ex-husband, hating that he was still in Katelyn's life when she should never have to see him again. She had been floating on a pleasant alcohol haze until then, but sobered up immediately as Aaron gazed at her, his jaw jutting out and his blue eyes boring into her. She knew he would get a kick out of the effect he was having on her and there was no way she was allowing him that, so she smiled widely and said, 'Say cheese,' and snapped the photo.

She hadn't known what would happen later. None of them

had. A sharp pain near her heart forces her to shift on the sofa. She wants to delete the photo but doesn't, just flicking past it quickly. Everything that happened after that moment – including telling Abigail and her group of sycophantic hangers-on that she was pregnant and not actually consuming any alcohol – happened later in the night, but when Leah thinks about it, everything can be traced back to the moment she took a picture of her ex-husband and Katelyn together and understood that something was going on between them. Nothing she could put her finger on, but something more than just a vague friend-ship with the man her husband was friends with.

'You and Aaron seem chummy,' Leah said, after the photo was done and Aaron was talking to Toby about football.

'Oh, he's... well, hey, let's get some more nachos,' said Kate-lyn, walking away before Leah even answered her.

Leah shakes her head and keeps scrolling. The photo of Aaron and Katelyn is followed by a couple of shots of Katelyn with preschool mothers and then one of Leah and Toby, obvi-ously taken by someone else but Leah can't remember who she handed her phone to. Toby has his arm around her and a giant grin on his face. He'd had a few drinks by then and really shouldn't have driven Katelyn to the hospital, but none of them were thinking straight. She and Toby look good together and, in another life, she could have been the one married to Toby with a gorgeous little girl. If she and Katelyn never speak again she will miss Harper terribly, but maybe she and Harper will see each other all the time anyway. She held the baby the day after she was born and she's seen her nearly every week of her life since then.

Toby thinks that Katelyn won't get her memory back, and that's what Leah has read as well, so the party can be erased and everything that happened there along with it, and she and Katelyn can just go back to being friends.

But that's not what Leah wants. She scrolls back to the

picture of Aaron and Katelyn, studying Aaron's face and remembering the first time she saw him. They met on Tinder and started chatting online but she was talking to at least three other men at the time and she was a seasoned dater, exhausted by the whole thing and bored with having to make superficial conversations with men who often had little to say for themselves. She nearly unmatched with Aaron because his answers to questions like 'How was your day?' and 'Where do you like to eat?' and 'How long have you been on the app?' were ridiculously monosyllabic. 'Fine.' 'Italian.' 'Not long.'

She only kept talking to him because he was so good-looking but after a few weeks she was done. There was a cute veterinarian she was talking to who loved *Lord of the Rings* and a slightly weird chef who collected spatulas, but at least they made conversation.

But then Aaron messaged her. *Can we meet. I suck at this chit-chat.* And she agreed and when she walked into the bar they had chosen and he stood up when he saw her, she wanted to giggle with relief that she had not unmatched him. In person he was charming, a little edgy and prone to getting angry, but she never minded that. He was thirty-eight and ready for marriage and at thirty-one, so was she. Their relationship progressed at breakneck speed. They should have had the big conversations before they got married. She should have checked that he would never budge on having kids, that he believed in fidelity, that his anger was controllable, that he was who she thought he was instead of someone else entirely.

Leah scrolls back to the picture of her and Toby and then she closes her eyes and tries to imagine what a child belonging to the two of them would look like. When she opens her eyes, she can feel the smile on her face and she gets off the sofa and goes to take a shower.

Once she's done, she sits at her small timber desk in the living room and opens every job website she can find. One day she will be a mother at home with her baby, and maybe a step-mother as well, but until then she needs a job and so she starts clicking and she gets to work.

After an hour, she's applied for ten new jobs and feels more positive, more able to deal with what's ahead of her. She changes into her running gear and puts on a playlist filled with house music that keeps her feet pounding the pavement as her mind turns over what she wants for her life and exactly how she plans to get it.

She focuses on an image of Katelyn's kitchen, sees the lovely marble countertop and Harper sitting at the small kitchen table colouring in. In her fantasy, Toby walks through the door and up to a woman standing at the counter, making a salad, her stomach rounded with pregnancy, and when the woman turns it is Leah's own face she sees, not Katelyn's face, Leah's body Toby wraps his arms around, not Katelyn's, Leah's life – just waiting to begin.

FOURTEEN

Katelyn and Leah – Thirty-Two Years Old

Leah spots Katelyn sitting at a table by the window, her eyes roaming up and down the menu even though she's going to order an iced coffee and a Caesar salad like she always does. In the café a heater blasts away the August winter chill and Leah shrugs off her inky-black coat, holding it in her hands. She moves through the tables swiftly, aware that other diners in the café are gazing at her. She's overdressed for lunch in a café but she has a dinner tonight and no time to go home. In her tight black dress with the low-cut back she feels exposed and judged, so she throws her shoulders back and lifts her head, flicking her blonde hair over her shoulder. Let them look.

Katelyn is dressed in her usual grey pants suit, an outfit she has worn for years, alternating it with other suits of a similar cut and colour. Katelyn prefers to blend in at work, but Leah needs to stand out now that she's marketing director. The We Adore You make-up site has grown so big she now has a team under her, a gaggle of enthusiastic young men and women who see her as impossibly glamorous and as having the answer for everything. Sometimes it helps Leah to see herself as they do, especially when she is questioning her decisions about her life.

'There you are, don't you look amazing,' says Katelyn as Leah gets to the table.

'Why, thank you,' laughs Leah, giving a little curtsy for effect.

'Please tell me you're going to get something to eat. I'm starving but it doesn't look like you can eat anything in that.'

'Actually,' says Leah, sitting down, 'it's more comfortable than it looks. I have a dinner later and no time to get home. It's so good to see you,' she says, reaching over and clasping Katelyn's hand. 'It feels like we never do anymore.'

'I know.' Katelyn's eyes darken as she shakes her head. 'It's just been... you know, but I have some news.'

'Me too, me too,' says Leah.

'Okay, you first,' says Katelyn.

'No, you.'

'I'm pregnant, three months, and I had a scan yesterday and everything looks perfect, according to my doctor.' She claps her hands with glee, looking so much like the six-year-old girl Leah remembers that she can't help laughing at her.

'Yay,' she says, clapping as well.

'I can't believe it,' says Katelyn, touching her eyes where tears have appeared.

'Oh, Kate,' says Leah and she squeezes Katelyn's hand as a lump forms in her throat. 'I'm so happy for you. I know it's been hideous, but why didn't you tell me before this?'

A waitress arrives before Katelyn can reply and Leah listens as she orders her usual, but an iced chocolate instead of the coffee, swiping quickly at her face, and then Leah orders the chicken salad and a glass of Prosecco. 'I'll celebrate for both of us,' she says as the waitress walks away, her tone bright to cover her dismay at not being included, at only hearing about the pregnancy now that Katelyn is three months along. Katelyn has told her how difficult it has been to fall pregnant and Leah knew that she and Toby were doing IVF, but she has deliberately not asked about it, reasoning that Katelyn will tell her when she's ready. Since Katelyn married Toby, she has been completely absorbed into his family and his life, embracing Maureen and Ted and celebrating being part of a family. Leah's parents are no longer as necessary in Katelyn's life as they once were and Leah knows her mother is hurt by this, but Leah is also hurt, having felt locked out of the exclusive Katelyn and Toby circle since they got married.

And once Katelyn started IVF, it has felt as though they have less in common than they ever did. Katelyn hates her job and does the bare minimum to get by, but she threw herself into the IVF community as though she were auditioning for the role of director of every single blog. There was nothing she didn't read and no group she didn't join and over the past year and a half her conversation has been littered with references to Monica and Janet and Selena and so many other names, and every time Leah has asked her about them, she has been told, 'Just a friend who knows what this is like.' And because Katelyn has been suffering and Leah has been able to see the strain on her friend's face, she has allowed the hurtful comment to pass. Now she wonders if the other women Katelyn has become friends with knew from the moment the pregnancy test was positive. She imagines they did. IVF feels like an exclusive club, however awful a club it is, and because Leah is not part of it, she has no right to be included in Katelyn's life anymore. She swallows down the hurt and grins at her friend. 'I am so happy for you,' and Katelyn nods.

'You've been such a support, you know. It was always a relief to go out with you and hear about your glamorous life.'

Leah laughs. 'I'm not sure my one hundred hours in the

office every week counts as glamorous but tonight is a dinner at the Intercontinental in the city, so that should be good.'

'Lucky you. Now tell me your news,' says Katelyn, as the waitress returns with their drinks.

Leah has rested her coat on her lap and now she takes her left hand out and shows Katelyn. 'Aaron proposed last night with this and I said, "Yes."'

The diamond on her left hand is large and square, surrounded by smaller diamonds and set in platinum.

'Oh my God,' breathes Katelyn. 'That's spectacular. I'm so happy for you. Are you happy?'

Leah nods and takes a sip of her drink, sitting back as the waitress returns with their food.

'You have to tell me everything,' says Katelyn, immediately tucking into her food. She can't believe how hungry she is these days. In the morning she can't imagine eating a single bite of food as the nausea sends her running for the bathroom first thing, but after that she thinks about food all day. 'I'm going to get so fat,' she moaned to Toby, but she had said the words with a smile on her face.

'I don't care if you gain a hundred kilos,' Toby said, 'as long as bubs is healthy and strong.'

Over the past six years, she and Toby have been trying to get pregnant for at least four. They thought that the minute they started trying it would happen and Katelyn had anticipated quitting her job with glee, knowing that it would not be long until she was home with a baby and she could be the kind of mother she never had. But even as their couple friends announced babies one after the other, she and Toby struggled. And now finally, after three rounds of IVF, 'bubs' is on the way. Katelyn is elated and terrified every minute of the day. She cannot wait to hold her baby in her arms. Every morning she wakes and lies in bed waiting for the nausea, anticipating it with glee and some fear in case it doesn't come. But every morning it's there and even as she throws up, she is filled with joy.

Together, she and Toby had decided to wait to tell anyone aside from those in their IVF community struggling along with them, and Maureen and Ted, of course. It was hard keeping quiet about it but they had to, knowing how precarious the situation was, and then yesterday when she got the all clear, the first call she had made was to Leah but all she got was her message bank. Leah is carving a swathe through the business world, leading a large team and making her mark. Katelyn had never anticipated that her own studies would not lead her to her dream career.

'It's okay to just want to be a mother,' Toby told her when they first started discussing having children.

'I feel like I've failed. I was supposed to run a gallery and live overseas, travel the world. But all I want to do is stay here with you and your family and have my own children,' Katelyn confessed.

'Then that's what we'll do,' laughed Toby, but he hadn't been aware of how hard it would be. Finally, they are here and while she would like to tell Leah every detail now, she knows that Leah's news needs her attention, even if she believes her friend is making a terrible mistake. Aaron is good-looking, really good-looking, tall and muscular with a square jaw and his own security firm, but there is something about the man that Katelyn finds scary. Toby thinks he's fabulous because Aaron has contacts everywhere and has taken Toby to sit in lavishly appointed boxes for the rugby and the cricket and the tennis. 'He's a good bloke, generous, and just down to earth. Leah is lucky to have found him,' Toby has said. In the year they have known each other the men have formed a close friendship.

But Katelyn always feels like Aaron is looking at her

strangely, like he's studying her to find her weak spots, and also like he doesn't respect the fact that she goes to work just to go to work.

'Your job should be your passion,' he said the first time they met over dinner. 'It is for me and I know it is for Leah as well,' and then he had maintained eye contact with her as he lifted his glass of red wine and took a deep sip. Katelyn had felt a flush creep up over her face and looked away first.

Katelyn would have been fine with Aaron not finding her that interesting if not for his temper. There have been more than a few occasions over the last year of Leah and Aaron dating when Leah has called her from her car. 'I'm just getting myself a coffee while he works his mood out,' she will tell Katelyn, regardless of whether it's 10 p.m. or 10 a.m.

'Come on, tell me every detail,' she says, looking up from her salad.

Leah smiles and Katelyn can see her pausing for effect so the whole story can be properly appreciated. 'So he rented out an entire restaurant, I mean it was just Romeo's, you know that small Italian place near where we live, but it's our favourite so he rented the whole thing out and I thought it was just because it was our first anniversary since we started dating. I bought him a Cartier watch and he loves it and I was waiting for my gift, but then he got down on one knee and I swear I nearly cried. I can't believe it, can you?'

Leah is breathless with happiness, her cheeks pink and her beautiful skin glowing and Katelyn knows this is not the time to voice anything other than joy for her. 'I am so happy for you both. I hope you won't mind a fat bridesmaid.'

'You won't be fat and you're my matron of honour so you can choose whatever you want to wear. We want to get married in two months. My mother has freaked out completely because it's too soon to plan a wedding, but Aaron is thirty-nine and I'm thirty-two and we want to be married as soon as possible.'

Katelyn takes another mouthful of salad as she watches her friend. 'And have you resolved the question of babies?' she asks quietly, unable to keep herself from saying something.

Leah shrugs. 'You know. He doesn't want kids and I think I might want them, but I'm not certain and I'm not willing to throw away the best relationship I've ever had over the issue. I'll be a fabulous aunt to your kids. I hope you're ready for me to spoil this little boy or girl rotten. Do you know what it is yet? Have you picked names? Ted and Maureen must be over the moon.'

Katelyn knows that Leah has shifted the conversation back to her for a reason. If Leah doesn't want to discuss something she turns the spotlight on those around her and she's very good at making a person feel like they are the most interesting thing she's seen all day, so people inevitably follow her lead. It's why she's so successful at work.

The relationship between Leah and Aaron is a puzzle to Katelyn because in his company, Leah seems less like herself rather than better than herself, as Katelyn feels she is with Toby. But Leah loves Aaron and so they will get married and probably have a fabulous life filled with travel and luxury. Katelyn wants nothing more than her little family.

'Oops, I seem to have finished my drink,' laughs Leah.

'But you've barely eaten anything.'

'Well…' Leah waves her hand. 'I'm having dinner with the CEO of the company tonight. He's coming in from Hong Kong and everyone is in a tizz because he wants to expand into the USA. It's going to be incredible because – and please don't say anything – I think I may be up for a promotion to managing director if Macy moves to the US to open the new division.'

'Oh, Leah, that's fabulous. And just to help you look your best, I'll finish your chicken salad. Bubs likes to eat constantly.'

'And I'll get another drink and we can discuss you coming with me and Mum to buy my dress. I'm thinking skintight and satin.' She flicks her hands and lifts a shoulder, the large diamond on her finger glinting in the weak sun coming through the café window.

'Perfect,' says Katelyn because of course it will be. Everything Leah does is perfect.

FIFTEEN

KATELYN

It's 1 p.m. and Toby has called her four times already from work, each time making her recount the day and the time, quizzing her on stupid things like who the prime minister of Australia is.

'Can you just stop?' she yelled at him on the fourth phone call.

'I'm sorry, I'm so sorry, Kate. I'm just worried that it will happen again and you're supposed to get Harper...'

Katelyn had taken a deep breath. 'It's okay. I know you're worried. But your calls are stressing me out and stress is probably what made the TGA happen in the first place.'

'Maybe,' said Toby but he sounded guarded, cagey.

'I wish you would just tell me what you're hiding, Toby,' she said, unable to keep the exasperation out of her voice. *Are you cheating on me? Are you sleeping with another woman, or even my best friend? Did you buy underwear for another woman? Did you buy it for me because you're unsatisfied with our sex life? Is our marriage okay?* The questions were on the tip of her tongue but she held them back. She needed more evidence of something actually going on, more than just an image of Leah and Toby hugging and underwear with a card addressed to no one.

'Oh God, for the millionth time, I am not hiding anything. It was a nice party and then you just...'

'I know, I know,' she said. 'You don't have to explain it again. I know what day it is and I know what time it is and I know I have to get Harper at 3 p.m. from Miss Ellen's class and the school is ten minutes' drive away. I have not lost my memory and I'm fine and I will text you when I'm on my way and when I have her and when I'm home. If I don't text you by two thirty, just call me then, okay? Otherwise, you should probably get some work done.' Katelyn took a deep breath when she finished speaking, hoping that her husband would accept that she was okay.

'Okay,' he said and she could hear the relief in his voice but she wasn't sure if it was because she had stopped asking what happened at the party, or because she had said she would text him when she went to fetch Harper.

She has also spoken to Maureen and tonight, after she and Harper open all her gifts, she will reply to everyone who has texted her and thank them for coming. She is looking forward to seeing Harper, to sitting with her little girl and hearing about her sleepover at her grandparents', and to watching her delight as she gets to unwrap all of Katelyn's presents. She misses Harper when she's not with her but, at the same time, it has been a huge relief to have this time to herself. Every time she drops Harper at preschool, a nagging feeling of guilt tugs at her as she leaves because she's so relieved to have the day alone. She loves her child and she reminds herself of that all the time. She's a good mother and she loves her child, but she has a right to a life beyond raising a child and that's why she doesn't want another baby. If someone had asked her when she was pregnant how many children she wanted she would have answered, 'As many as I get to have.' But wanting a child and having a child are two very different things.

Aaron has agreed to meet for lunch. In the last three months she has met Aaron for lunch a number of times and found him easy to talk to and very supportive. She wouldn't exactly call them friends but she likes him more now than she did when he was married to Leah. She is no longer scared of him, able to see his slightly brusque demeanour as just the way he is.

The café is one close to Katelyn's home. Despite what she's said to Toby, she feels unsure about venturing too far from home. What if she loses her memory again and ends up lost? The doctor said it won't happen again but the doctor also didn't know what caused it. The niggle of worry over what happened to her is a continuous loop of what ifs.

She has driven slowly and carefully over to the café, making sure to pay close attention to the traffic. It's a grey day with clouds low and threatening but so far it hasn't rained, for which she is grateful.

As she manoeuvres into a parking spot, she remembers her first solo lunch with Aaron three months ago. She had asked him to keep their meetings secret, not wanting to talk to Toby until everything was in place.

It's an idea that never would have even occurred to Katelyn if she hadn't found herself alone with Aaron one Saturday night as Toby read Harper a bedtime story.

Since his divorce from Leah, Katelyn had made it a priority to stay out of the way when Aaron came over, going out, or just being upstairs when he and Toby spent time together. Mostly they met outside of the house, or at Aaron's place.

'You should stop being friends with him,' Katelyn told Toby when they first learned that Leah and Aaron were planning to get divorced.

'I know that's what you want,' said Toby, 'but actually, he's basically my best mate now and I don't have a lot of friends. We get on really well. I asked Leah and she said she's okay with it.'

'When did you ask Leah?' Katelyn said, a leftover sting of jealousy causing her to sound angry.

'We talk, Kate, you know we do. I called her to tell her how sorry I was and I asked her. It's important to me. I don't want to have to give up seeing him. We're adults and it's not like he cheated on her or anything.'

'No, but the way he asked for a divorce wasn't nice and you know what's happened with the apartment,' Katelyn argued.

'Listen,' Toby sighed. 'They just weren't right for each other but you know Leah, she'll have someone else in her life soon enough. I asked her and she said it was fine. She even told me that they're trying to be cordial about things.'

'I still don't like it and I know she doesn't either. She just wants us to believe that she's fine, that the two of them are doing some sort of conscious uncoupling rubbish, but she's not,' Katelyn huffed but Toby was adamant and his friendship with Aaron had only gotten stronger.

They went to the football, met for drinks and dinner and played tennis every couple of weeks. Katelyn had, in fact, seen very little of Aaron and certainly less than she thought she would.

But three months ago, Aaron's internet wasn't working and there was an important football match on and so he ended up in their living room on a Saturday night and Katelyn was happier to sit with him than to be reading Harper five bedtime stories.

'I won't be long,' Toby said, giving her a reassuring glance as Harper tugged him by the hand.

'I want the one about the grumpy monkey, Daddy, the grumpy monkey and you have to do the voice,' Harper said. Katelyn closed her eyes briefly. She had spent the whole day with Harper shopping for new shoes and having lunch and she needed some time out.

Aaron had brought a bottle of good red wine and he poured a glass for Katelyn. 'Looks like you could use this,' he said, handing her the glass.

Katelyn nodded, scooting closer to him on the sofa to take the glass. 'I could,' she sighed. 'This is good,' she said after the first sip.

'Yeah,' agreed Aaron. 'I got it from a small bottle shop in the city. I never even knew it was there but it's filled with the best wine and the guy who owns it is so picky about what he stocks and he really wants to choose something for you that will go with your meal, it's a whole thing,' he said, waving his hand.

'It's like a backlash against the giant corporate bottle shops,' said Katelyn.

'It is, it feels like it's going on everywhere. There are small bars and galleries and restaurants down alleyways, it's great.'

'I wanted to run a gallery,' said Katelyn, her body loosened from the wine.

'Then you should,' said Aaron and he reached over and topped up her glass. 'You hated your job but it had nothing to do with your art history degree. You should do something you love. And I know that there's no way you're stimulated enough just taking care of Harper. Don't get me wrong, it's great but I've always thought you were wasting your talents and intelligence at your old job. Harper's going to go to school soon and you should have something for yourself.'

Katelyn took another sip of wine to cover her surprise. Aaron had articulated exactly the way she felt but didn't want to say. She craved something more than just taking care of Harper, but she never felt she could explain this to Toby after everything she had said before having a child.

'You thought I was intelligent,' she said, looking at Aaron, focusing on his deep-blue eyes and not looking away. 'I always thought you believed I wasn't very smart.'

Aaron's deep laugh made her smile. 'That's not what I

thought at all,' he said. 'You're the smartest out of the four of us, even Toby with his law degree knows that.'

Katelyn had felt her cheeks redden with pleasure at his words. Toby never asked her what she thought about anything, other than domestic concerns and Harper. If she tried asking him about his cases, he always told her everything was confidential.

'You should open a gallery,' he said. 'You wouldn't need a big space and I know there's always stuff to lease around the city.'

'I would have no idea where to even start; I mean I know what I like but I've only worked in that world as an intern. When I graduated, I couldn't find a job in the art world.'

'I know someone who runs a gallery,' Aaron said and Katelyn put down her wine glass and looked at him.

'You do?'

'I do, but she's moving to New Zealand so she's going to shut it down or sell it.' He shrugged like it was no big deal but to Katelyn it felt like the universe was speaking directly to her.

'Imagine if I could buy it,' she breathed, excitement making her heart race as she thought of finally having something that she owned, that she was good at. She thought about finally being Katelyn the woman and not just Katelyn the mother, or Katelyn the worker bee with no interest in what she was doing.

Aaron smiled at her, finished his glass and poured himself another and then sat forward, closer to her, and she couldn't help noticing just how nice he smelled, something subtle and earthy. She found herself staring at him and then dropped her eyes and finished her own glass of wine, knowing that she would get sleepy really soon.

'Well, the funny thing is, I've been wanting to invest in something like a gallery but now that she's leaving, I thought I'd lost the chance.' He spoke slowly, almost seductively.

And just like that, Katelyn's body was alive with adrenaline and possibility.

As she gets out of her car, she thinks about that night and the whispered conversation she and Aaron had as they agreed to meet to discuss the possibility of Katelyn buying the gallery from Liza, with Aaron's help.

'What are you two discussing?' Toby had laughed when he came downstairs from putting Harper to bed.

'Oh, the wine,' Aaron said and he had launched into his whole story about the small wine store as Katelyn stood up, throwing him a grateful look for knowing that she wasn't ready to discuss the idea with Toby yet without her even having to say anything. Aaron is perceptive and clever.

In the past few months, she and Aaron have met with Liza and then with each other, discussing every aspect of the business. She only wanted to tell Toby once she and Aaron had a plan in place and she had worked out how to be there for Harper and work.

Her plan was to discuss the idea with Toby after her birthday party but the idea of opening her own gallery feels impossible now. Toby would be completely against it and she knows that what happened to her memory will be used by Toby as the first reason why she shouldn't go back to work. The fact that he wants another child will also be on his list. Katelyn can hear his argument against the gallery before he even says a word and she can feel the resentment inside her at his being able to control her life in any way. She needs to be clearer and stronger first so she can counter his arguments. Perhaps in a few weeks she'll feel better and she hopes that Aaron is happy to wait.

She walks into the café and sees Aaron sitting at a table at the back and waves. If Aaron told Toby what the two of them have been doing on the night of the party, she knew her husband would be angry with her for keeping something so big from him, especially since they will have to invest a fair amount of money. But why not just say something? An image of Toby and Leah together assaults her and she blinks quickly, ridding herself of the picture as she sits down at the table opposite Aaron.

'I've never been here,' says Aaron, sitting back in his chair. 'It's nice.' Katelyn looks around at the walls decorated with moody black-and-white landscape photographs and typical timber tables in the café. 'Leah hates it here,' she says. 'It reminds her of some suburban nightmare with all the mothers and their kids.'

The café is relatively quiet because it's just after the lunch rush when all the toddlers and their mothers have left for an afternoon nap. 'They have good food. I'm just going to get a sandwich,' she says.

A waitress comes over and they both order roast beef sandwiches and water to drink. 'I wish we were somewhere nicer,' says Aaron.

Katelyn shrugs. She doesn't want to tell him about her memory loss but she has to if she wants him to tell her the truth.

'Have you talked to Leah since Saturday night?' Her hands move the salt and pepper shakers back and forth, nerves making her fidgety.

'Nah,' he says, looking up and smiling at the waitress as she puts down the two sandwiches. The waitress smiles back and blushes slightly. Aaron is a good-looking man.

'Okay, I'm going to... look... I...' She doesn't know how to begin.

'I know what you're going to say,' he says as he swallows a bite of sandwich.

'You do?' she says, lifting her sandwich and taking a bite.

'You're upset about Toby.' Katelyn looks at him, and he nods his head as though he knows there's a reason she should be upset about Toby. The underwear returns to haunt her and she pairs it with the image she has of Leah and Toby hugging.

Aaron's nod seems to indicate that what she suspects is true and her heart drops, her throat closing over.

'I am, I mean... of course, he and Leah...' She stops speaking, not wanting to say the words, not wanting to make it real but Aaron cannot be talking about anything else.

'Don't worry about Leah.' He takes another bite of his sandwich and then wipes his mouth on a paper serviette, dismissing Leah with a shake of his head. How can he tell her that? If he really knows what happened then how can he say something like that? He sounds completely unbothered by the idea of Toby and Leah having an affair and maybe that's because he's no longer married to Leah.

Katelyn puts down her sandwich, struggling to swallow her bite and then taking a large sip of water to help. This can't be true. She doesn't want it to be true and she doesn't want Aaron to say the words but she needs to hear them. Inside her is a tiny flicker of hope that she has misunderstood Aaron, that maybe she is entirely wrong about Leah and Toby. That's the best-case scenario. She's wrong and Toby found out about her plan to buy the gallery and that's what happened at the party. It doesn't explain her memory loss though. Finding out her husband was having an affair would, however, explain it. Stress can cause a TGA.

She will ask Aaron exactly what he knows and then she will drive to Toby's office and confront him. Her life feels like it's hanging perilously in the balance, her safe world about to drop off a precipice, but this will be all the evidence she needs.

She tries to take another bite of her sandwich, but she can't. Dropping the sandwich back onto her plate, she wipes her fingers and takes a deep breath.

'Aaron, on Saturday night I had something, like a kind of episode, and I lost my memory for the whole of Sunday,' she explains, quickly looking around her when she's done in case one of the mothers from Harper's preschool has suddenly wandered in without her noticing.

Aaron sits back and laughs. 'You're so funny,' he says.

Katelyn lays both her palms flat on the tabletop, wrinkling her nose at the stickiness. 'I'm not being funny. I lost my memory and Toby had to take me to hospital. It's something called TGA and it's a kind of amnesia brought on by stress, or diving into cold water or even' – she shakes her head – 'orgasm,' she says, flushing at saying the word to Aaron. 'No one knows a lot about it, but it happened to me and I seem to have not only lost Sunday but I'm also sure that something happened at the party that I just can't remember. So, I wanted to know if you remember something, something between me and Toby, or me and Leah, an argument or something, just anything. Even something between Toby and Leah,' she finishes softly, knowing what he will say, completely sure he will not say anything else.

She has been staring down at her hands as she speaks, moving her fingers slightly on the sticky table so she doesn't have to look at him, but when she's done she lifts her eyes to meet his gaze.

'You're joking, right?' he says. 'I mean, you absolutely have to be joking.' He leans forward and wraps one of his big hands around her wrist. 'Tell me you're joking, Katelyn,' he spits.

She pulls back, sudden shock and fear running through her blood. 'Aaron,' she says, her voice a whisper because she can already feel the few people in the café staring at them. 'What's wrong with you? I'm not joking. It really happened and I thought you might remember something that could help me, but if you're going to get weird, I'll go.' She doesn't want to know this, doesn't want to face the truth right now. She'll ask Toby tonight. It's wrong to speak to Aaron before she has confronted Toby.

She starts to stand up.

'Sit. Down.' The words are clipped with anger.

Katelyn drops back into her chair, unsure what to do and not wanting to cause a scene. Aaron has a commanding voice and presence. He seems to be really angry at her, but why?

'You don't just get to pretend with me, Katelyn, not with me.'

'Aaron,' she says, her head beginning to throb with confusion. 'I'm not pretending. I just want to understand.' This was a terrible idea. Alarm bells are ringing in her head.

Aaron leans forward, close to her, too close. 'What happened, Katelyn, lovely sweet Katelyn, is that you and I had sex.'

He sits back in his chair, folds his arms across his broad chest and stares at her. 'We had sex,' he repeats, loud enough for everyone in the café to hear.

'S... E... X,' he spells out while she stares at him.

'And actually,' he continues with a smile, 'you quite enjoyed it.'

SIXTEEN

LEAH

Tuesday Afternoon – Three Days After the Party

She has paid special attention to how she dresses, taking time with her make-up and sliding into a knitted sheath dress in chocolate brown. It's paired with a cream wool coat to keep out the cold.

In the city she walks quickly with her head down against the icy wind that always seems to fill up the streets, as she makes her way to Toby's law firm. Toby wants to forget and move on, but the only way she's going to let that happen is if she is the one who gets amnesia.

Toby's law firm is housed in one of the smaller buildings in the city, along with an accountancy firm and a psychology practice, which is probably handy for those who need to see Toby.

It's an older style red-brick building with timber window frames, unlike the newer ones that are shaped with steel and glass. Inside the heating is turned up a little too high and the speckled blue carpet needs replacing. Leah has been here before when she needed to know what to expect from divorce. Then Toby had been kind and consoling, handing her one tissue after another as she cried in his office over her broken marriage. He had advised her to go through mediation before engaging a lawyer and then he recommended a colleague of his who could help. Marcia had been quick and efficient, calling Leah's divorce 'an easy fix' since she and Aaron didn't have children, and the only asset they had was their apartment, which was wholly owned by Aaron.

'Your name isn't on the deed. Did you know that?' Marcia asked, pushing her auburn hair behind her ears and then grabbing an elastic and tying it back.

'Well, he already had the apartment when we got married and I'm sure there was some discussion about putting my name on the deed but...' Leah had stopped speaking, feeling herself flush with embarrassment. In the three years she and Aaron had been married she hadn't really thought about her financial position. She bought groceries and he paid for everything else. That should have meant that she was accumulating a lot of money since she earned a nice salary but Leah loved beautiful things, buying designer handbags and shoes with abandon. Self-consciously she had clutched her Gucci tote bag. She had never bought a place before marrying Aaron, content to pay rent and enjoy her money and now she was thirty-five with a small amount of savings and a collection of bags and shoes, but no husband or child. Despair had settled over her and Marcia had let the silence grow before saying, 'Look, you're young. You'll start again. You'll get there.' But Leah hadn't felt young. She had felt old and tired and a failure.

Shaking off the memory, Leah reminds herself to stick to her plan. She can start again and she can do it better this time.

Toby's firm is on the third floor and Leah gets into the elevator with a couple who stand as far apart from each other as possible. The woman stands in one corner, a tissue clutched in her hand as she sniffs occasionally. The man mutters, 'For God's sake,' quietly.

The elevator is old and creaks its way slowly up to the third floor and Leah remembers Katelyn saying that Toby's firm are getting ready to move somewhere bigger and newer.

This morning she had texted Toby first thing, asking him if he was going to work and if she should come and sit with Katelyn.

Toby hadn't replied but Katelyn had replied to the text she sent her. *Thanks, Toby is going in today but I'm fine. I know you have work so please don't worry. Maureen is around if I need her x*

She couldn't exactly reply that she didn't have work so she returned the message with *xx*. Something about the message felt different, more formal than the way she and Katelyn usually texted each other, but she was glad to know that Toby was going in to work.

On the third floor she and the couple get out and for about the tenth time today, Leah wonders if she should do what she's about to do. But every time she thinks this, she decides that she has every right to look after her own happiness. Toby wants to just forget about everything that happened at the party, but Leah can never forget.

At the door to Toby's offices the couple stop and turn to look at her. She ducks her head, and then the man opens the door and they all go in together into the hushed carpeted area of reception where the sadness of the situation seems reflected in the dark panelled walls and black leather sofas. 'We're here to see Marcia Wallace,' says the man softly to the receptionist whose name is something like Jill or Jane, Leah can't remember, but she's sure few people remember the name of the receptionist in the office of a group of divorce lawyers. Leah stands quietly while the receptionist calls Marcia to let her know her clients have arrived.

'If you could just take a seat, she'll be right out,' says the receptionist and the couple sit on separate sofas, both immediately taking out their phones.

The couple are older and Leah imagines that they have children and a whole life together to pick apart, although she has no idea why they have come together. Perhaps they are just starting the process and have no idea what to do.

Aaron didn't even engage a lawyer, just said, 'I'll pay you half what it costs to draw everything up, let's get this done.' He wanted her out of his life as quickly as she had entered it. Neatly stowed away like he did with all his socks.

'Please,' she had begged, 'can we just talk about it some more?' but Aaron was immovable.

'Can I help you?' the receptionist asks once she is done with the older couple.

'I'm here to see Toby, Tobias Abbot,' she says.

'Give me a moment, I didn't have an appointment for him for this afternoon.'

'Oh, I don't have one, I'm a... friend. Leah.' The receptionist nods and then makes a call, speaks quietly into her phone.

At the end of the hall, a dark timber door opens and Toby strides out, looking slightly flustered. 'Leah, is everything okay?' he asks, before he notices the older couple who are both looking at her now.

'I just wanted to talk,' she says and he nods and turns, heading back to his office as Leah follows him.

'What's up?' he asks as he shuts the door and Leah touches her stomach to quiet the twisting as she remembers the last time she sat here. Toby's desk is clean, with only his laptop open and a pad of paper next to it, the pen lying at a neat angle across the paper. Leah had hoped for a casual greeting, for some easy conversation but she can see she's not going to get that.

'I wanted to talk about the party, about what you're going to tell Katelyn,' she says.

Toby drops into his black swivel chair and crosses his arms

over his chest. 'I thought you understood that I don't want to say anything at all.'

'Well, I think that's wrong.' He hasn't asked her to sit down but she does, leaning forward and resting her hands in her lap. 'Don't you want to know the truth?' she asks.

'What does that mean? Were you lying to me?' He narrows his eyes and leans forward. He's suspicious of her now but there is also some hope in his gaze. He wants her to have lied to him. He loves his wife. He shouldn't. Katelyn doesn't deserve someone like Toby.

Leah removes her coat, suddenly boiling. She's sure she had a plan for how this conversation was supposed to go. 'I could call her now and tell her what I saw so you can hear what she says and maybe she'll remember it all.'

'What? Why?' Toby slaps his hands down on his desk. 'I just want to move on. I don't want to think about it ever again. She lost her memory. It's over and I want it to be over. And if you speak to her, you could trigger another event. The doctor said she had to avoid any stress for a few days. You're her best friend, why would you want to do that to her?'

'Maybe she's faking it,' says Leah slowly. 'I mean... don't tell me you haven't considered that?'

Toby rubs his eyes under his glasses. 'She messed up but she was drunk and... I've been thinking that maybe you didn't really see what you thought you saw.' Now she can hear his hope and it doesn't just irritate her. It makes her furious.

Leah stands. 'Toby, you're such a pushover, such a doormat. I saw them, I caught them.'

He rubs at his head in frustration. 'I don't want to discuss it, I don't want to talk about it.' He raises his voice. 'I can't think about it anymore. I thought she was going to die, or that she had Alzheimer's or something awful like that. But she doesn't and I want to just... let it go and start again. She's been unhappy, you know that, but she was drunk and it didn't mean anything. I know it didn't mean anything.'

Leah can hear that Toby has been repeating these phrases to himself over and again since the party, that he has been trying to convince himself so that he can move on. He looks close to tears.

'Okay, okay, calm down.' She lifts her hands, needing him to lower his voice.

'I'm sorry, it's just... Harper is only three and she needs her mother. She has a right to grow up in a home with both parents. It was a mistake. I know it was a mistake and I don't want her to remember it.' He sounds needy, desperate for her to agree with him.

'Maybe you should ask Aaron.'

'You really think I'm ever talking to Aaron again?' Toby sneers.

'But don't you want to know the absolute truth? Don't you want to be sure? I mean, she cheated on you. I would want to know.'

'I don't want to know,' he says, slapping the desk again, baring his teeth.

'I'm sorry,' she says. 'You're right. You have to think about Harper.' She stands and shrugs on her coat again. She will need to find another way to get through to him. 'I just think it's so unfair. You're a good man, Toby. I wish I had known what a mistake it was to break up with you all those years ago and she doesn't appreciate you. She doesn't even appreciate Harper.'

Toby stands. 'You didn't break up with me,' he says and then he shakes his head. 'Leah, you have to let this go now. She's your... she's your best friend and she's my wife and we have to find a way to forgive her. It was a drunken mistake and I know that if she had remembered it, she would have said that. I know her, Leah. I can't break up my marriage over this.'

Leah is surprised at the anger that flows through her body, leading to hot tears. Why couldn't she have married a man like

Toby? She covers her mouth with her hand to stifle the embarrassing sounds she is making.

'Hey, hey, it's okay, it's okay,' says Toby, coming around his desk to stand next to her. He wraps her in a hug, holding tight. 'I know how hard this is for you and you've been amazing, you've always been amazing.'

Leah wraps her arms around his body, wondering how it still feels familiar to her after all this time and then she looks up at him, at his soft lips and his warm brown eyes and she cannot stop herself from touching his lips with hers.

This is what she came for, this is what she wanted and this is her new start. She loves Harper. They can be a family.

She feels his mouth move and then she feels his hands move onto her shoulders as he pushes her back. 'What are you doing?' he whispers furiously. 'What the hell are you doing?'

'I...' she says, but then cannot say anymore. He was supposed to respond, to kiss her back and then everything would have been fine. But he has rejected her again, once again.

A secret that she has never shared with Katelyn, never told anyone, and one that she has been grateful that Toby has held onto as well, is that she didn't break up with him. She would have stayed with Toby, would have married him if he asked, but she felt him pulling away over the months they were together and she saw how his eyes would light up every time he looked at Katelyn. She saw it but she didn't want to see it until one day when they were having what she regarded as a light-hearted conversation about marriage.

They were in Toby's sixth floor apartment with the glass doors open to an early evening summer breeze on a Friday night as they watched the city lights come on in one building after another. Toby's apartment was simple and spare with only a leather sofa, a coffee table and a bed in the bedroom. Leah had looked forward to helping him furnish it. They were sitting

together on the soft sofa, legs entwined, when he moved away
from her.

'Look,' he said. 'I need to be honest with you because I'm
not being fair to you. I feel like a terrible person but I'm
not... not ready to settle down with you.'

'That's okay. I'm not looking to get married now. It's just a
joke, Toby,' she said.

'No,' he replied, looking uncomfortable. 'I just don't think
the two of us work, you know. I like you. You're great but—'

Leah will never know how she put two and two together but
she had made the connection instantly. 'You're in love with
Katelyn,' she said and Toby had nodded miserably.

'I am but I promise you that I will not ask her out. I won't go
near her. I just didn't want to string you along. It's not fair to
you, Leah, you're amazing.'

Leah had been more resilient then, more able to control
herself in front of people so she pulled it together and said,
'That's fine, Toby, really. I was kind of thinking we were too
similar anyway. And you can date Katelyn. She's my best
friend. I want her to be happy.' She had finished her speech
with a bright smile to show how fine she was, even as her throat
choked up with the tears she knew she was going to shed.

'Maybe,' he said with a smile. 'You decide – you tell her
what you want. If she contacts me... but otherwise, I won't do
anything. You're lovely and I wish you a great life.'

'Of course,' Leah had mumbled. 'Oh my phone,' she said as
her phone buzzed with an incoming email. 'I forgot. I have
drinks with a friend. See you, Toby,' she had said gaily, kissing
him on the cheek. 'And good luck with Katelyn.'

She had left his apartment and run down the six flights of
stairs rather than take the elevator, not wanting to see anyone,
not wanting anyone else to witness her humiliation.

After half an hour of crying in her car, she had stopped off
at a bar with a country music theme and a mechanical bull in

the centre, fixed her make-up and let a nice guy chat her up and buy her drinks. She can't even remember his name now but by the time she got home, Katelyn had been asleep so she didn't have to see her. The next night she had waited until she would usually have been getting ready to go out with Toby to tell Katelyn and she had been able to change the story to suit her. It had been her idea. It's been so long since that happened that sometimes she forgets the truth but now, standing in Toby's office, rejected again, the ugly truth returns and like last time, all she wants is to get far away from him.

Picking up her coat, she opens the door to his office.

'You may want to forget what happened at the party, Toby, but I don't think Katelyn will be as quick to forget what happened when Harper was a baby,' she says, the words appearing in the air laced with anger.

'You wouldn't dare,' he whispers, conscious that the door is open to the reception area.

'I might,' she smirks. 'I'm sure she would be really interested to hear what happened.'

Almost instantaneously, Toby has moved to the door and he grasps her wrist, squeezing hard as he shuts the door with his other hand.

'Stop,' she says and he squeezes harder, making her wince at the strength in his hands.

'If you tell Katelyn what happened, I promise you, Leah Randall, I will make your life a living hell. I will make you sorry you even dreamed about opening your mouth and then when you are at your lowest, I will kill you.'

Leah gasps, unable to even recognise Toby's voice as his brown eyes darken with deep rage. Toby is not a frightening man, never has been, but Leah finds herself terrified and absolutely sure that he will make good on his promise.

His hand loosens around her wrist and she wrenches the door back open and runs out, not even caring that the receptionist gives her a quizzical glance. And once again she takes her rejection down the stairs, but after the first set of stairs she stops in the cold stairwell and vows that this time she's not going to just let Katelyn have everything she wants. She is so sick of being the one who loses. She hates Katelyn and Toby fiercely for a moment. She's not going to let this happen. She's not going to swallow her broken-hearted tears and just keep going.

This time it's going to end differently.

SEVENTEEN

How much has she had to drink? Too much. Way too much.

But she feels like she needs a lot more.

She has slipped the pregnancy test into her bag, knowing that it's something she can't think about right now. She simply cannot deal with it. *Stop drinking. You need to stop drinking.*

Skirting the edges of the party, she watches groups of people warily, trying to find a space for herself where she can safely just stand and smile and nod. She doesn't need to take any more pictures and she's just waiting for everyone to go home and for this to be over.

The news of Abigail's pregnancy is circulating the party now, women whispering the news to each other, big smiles from everyone, and she can see people gravitating towards the couple. Abigail with her hand on her flat belly, already protecting something precious. Leah unconsciously touches her own belly and then heads to the drinks table.

As she pours herself a drink she sees Katelyn head upstairs, her hands running through her hair to get it away from her neck. The house is overheated now with bodies, the smell of sweat and alcohol mingling.

Leah makes her way to the staircase but before she gets there, she sees Aaron going upstairs. Is he going to use the upstairs bathroom? She glances around the corner of the living room and sees two people standing outside the guest bathroom but is immediately resentful that Aaron feels he can just go upstairs in Katelyn and Toby's house. He should not be here, should never be invited here again, but she can't say that. Only hysterical, neurotic women who cannot move on from their exes say that.

Wanting to talk to Katelyn, to have a moment alone with her friend so they can have a discussion, she makes her way upstairs.

Katelyn is not in her bedroom. Leah looks around for a moment before a clunking sound from the bathroom startles her.

'Kate?' she says and when there is no reply she moves towards the bathroom.

'I don't... no,' she hears.

'You know you do, you know you do, oh my God, you're amazing,' she hears.

Freezing horror trickles through her body. That was Katelyn's voice and Aaron. Those voices belong to Katelyn and Aaron.

Her hand moves towards the door handle and she's shocked when it turns, shocked when the door simply opens and devastated at what she sees.

It isn't like a scene from the movies. There is nothing beautiful or sexy about it, just two people who should not be having sex, grappling with each other, making strange sounds. Katelyn's jeans are at her knees and Aaron's pants around his ankles. Her head is back against the mirror of the vanity cabinet as

Aaron holds her up on the marble top of the unit where a glass of something sweet smelling has spilled.

It is awful, degrading, so wrong.

Leah cannot muster a reaction. A strange giggle escapes her lips as her hand squeezes the door handle, her fingers cramping from the force she is using.

Aaron stops and turns towards her. 'Get out, get out, get out,' he hisses, murder in his eyes.

Leah's body reacts for her and she pulls the door closed with a slam, her heart racing, head pounding. Leaving the room, she walks straight into Toby.

'Oh hey, I was just looking for—'

'They're together,' she blurts. 'Together in the bathroom, Aaron and Katelyn, they're... oh God, Toby.'

'What? What are you talking about?'

The bedroom door opens behind her and Katelyn comes out, smoothing her hair, her silver silk blouse misbuttoned. Behind her is Aaron, tucking in his black shirt.

'What's going on?' asks Toby.

'Nothing,' says Katelyn and she walks past them as though nothing has happened, making her way downstairs.

Aaron steps right up to Leah, whispers in her ear, 'Bitch,' and then he follows Katelyn down the stairs.

'They were having sex,' Leah says to Toby whose face pales. 'Sex,' she repeats.

'They... weren't...' says Toby. 'It's not... they couldn't have been.'

'I'm sorry, Toby,' says Leah, stepping forward, offering a hug, feeling his arms around her.

'What are you two doing?' Katelyn calls from the bottom of the stairs. Toby steps away from her, and Leah sags, deprived of any comfort at all.

'Hey, it's the birthday girl,' a woman named Carol shouts.

She has wound some silver tinsel around her head and has a cocktail in one hand. 'Come on, birthday girl,' she sings to Katelyn. 'Time for cake,' and she grabs Katelyn's hand and pulls her away.

'Am I the birthday girl?' Katelyn yells above Justin Timberlake telling them to, *cry me a river*. 'Am I?'

'I can't deal with this now,' says Toby and he leaves Leah upstairs with only her devastation for company.

It is nearing the end of the party and she takes the steps slowly, listening to everyone sing 'Happy Birthday'. It's the first time in the last thirty years that she has not stood next to Katelyn when she blows out birthday candles.

She spots Abigail getting helped into her coat by her solicitous husband. All the things she doesn't have tumble around inside her and so she makes the decision to have just one thing.

'I wanted to tell you,' she says to Abigail, leaning forward and whispering into her ear, watching the woman smile. 'But it's a secret,' she says and Abigail nods.

'I won't tell a soul.'

Leah nods and accepts a hug from the woman who she doesn't care if she never sees again.

She's made a huge mistake saying anything at all and has no real idea why she did it. Abigail won't feel sorry for her now, or perhaps she will be sorrier for Leah because of the divorce.

Katelyn is standing next to the large chocolate frosted cake, eating a white icing rose.

'Something is wrong,' she says to Leah.

'Yes,' agrees Leah. 'Something is very wrong.'

Someone taps Katelyn on the shoulder to offer a hug goodbye and Leah steals into the kitchen to wait. She's not leaving until Katelyn explains, apologises, until she says something that will stop Leah wanting to kill her.

She's not leaving until then.

EIGHTEEN

KATELYN AND LEAH – THIRTY-THREE
YEARS OLD

'Should we knock again?' asks Leah, moving the bag of takeaway Thai food to her other hand.

'Maybe, I don't know,' says Aaron. 'Toby said she goes insane if anyone wakes the baby. But screw it.' He lifts his hand and she grabs his fist before it connects with the door.

'Please don't,' she says, quickly realising she's made a mistake.

'Leah.' He lowers his fist and turns to look at her. 'Don't grab me. Don't ever grab me, okay.'

Leah drops her gaze to her fabulous suede boots and nods. 'Sorry,' she whispers. It is easier to apologise, easier to back down. If she told this fact to anyone who knew her they would laugh and question what had happened to her mind. They've only been married for seven months but already the lavish wedding ceremony at a hotel in the city with one hundred and fifty guests and a jazz band seems very far away. Sometimes Leah scrolls through the wedding pictures on her Instagram and wonders if the beautiful bride she was had even a small inkling of how difficult Aaron would be to live with. Something she's only recently picked up on is that in most of the pictures of the two of them she is looking at Aaron, but he is looking at the camera. Leah had imagined that she was the star of the show but perhaps Aaron had imagined the same thing and relationships didn't do well with two stars – every failed Hollywood marriage made that clear.

'You seem a lot quieter lately, darling,' her mother said yesterday when they were talking about meeting up for dinner on Saturday night.

'What do you mean by that?' Leah asked, acid in her throat as instant anger churned inside her.

'Nothing, nothing, I just mean... when we see you and Aaron, you're... Look, never mind. Is there anything bothering you? You can talk to me, you know you can.'

'It's nothing, Mum. I'm fine, just busy. It's hard work managing my team and the CEO is calling every week from Hong Kong to question sales because revenue has dropped a little and... God, you don't want to hear this. I'm even boring myself.' Her dream career, her huge job, had become a noose around her neck. She was still head of marketing because a new general manager had been brought in when Marcia went to the US, but now it seemed that every time sales were less than stellar, everyone looked right at her. She understood because she was marketing but a changing landscape, more and more websites appearing, and economic woes all over the world, also had to be factored in. With alarming regularity she wished she could just walk away, just be home with a child, just be like Katelyn.

'I do want to hear it,' her mother said, dragging Leah back into her phone conversation, 'and you can tell us all about it on Saturday night.'

Leah knew that she would end up cancelling her parents for tomorrow night. It's what usually happened. Or she would have to go alone. Aaron thinks that her father doesn't like him, that he finds him rude and aggressive, and Leah knows without even asking her father that it's true.

Before they married, Aaron had been what a lot of people would call 'spiky'. He was quick to anger and often took innocuous comments the wrong way. But anytime Leah confronted him about yelling at someone, or questioning her father's motivation in asking him about his work, or her mother's questions about his family, he would immediately get defensive and the conversation would inevitably find its way back to his time spent in the army, serving in Afghanistan and everything he had seen and done there. Leah had no doubt that Aaron's time overseas was traumatic and that he still suffered the after-effects of war, but she also understood now that he used that time to excuse a lot of his behaviour. He no longer spoke to any of his old army buddies, not wanting to talk to anyone who reminded him of his time in the service.

'No one wants to think about that,' he told her if she broached the subject. 'Our lives there were not like the movies, don't romanticise any of it – it was war and it was awful. And you will never know what it was like.'

'But I would like to know. I want to understand what you went through,' she countered once or twice.

'Stop. Just stop,' was his usual reply and then he would walk away, leave the apartment and disappear for hours.

'Maybe counselling would help,' she has suggested more than once, only to have him look at her with such pure hatred in his eyes that she feels the need to get away from him.

'I don't need that. If you loved me enough, you would understand that. I don't need someone delving into my brain. I can think of nothing worse.'

It's not that he's like this all the time, not at all. She is mostly happy with him and their life. They live in the beautiful apartment Aaron bought before he met her with a lovely view of the harbour and they go out to dinner nearly every night. They are

invited to the best parties because he is usually the one
providing security for events. They are a 'golden couple', as one
site on the internet dubbed them. It's just that when they are
alone at home together, she finds herself watching what she
says. He always has a lot of advice on what she should say and
do at work, but if she makes a single comment on his work he
sneers, 'And what would you know about keeping people safe,
princess?'

He likes to be in charge, likes to be the biggest, smartest man
in the room. And when they are out together, Leah cannot miss
the envious looks other women throw her way. Aaron is good-
looking and successful. She should be ecstatic to be with him.
And Toby, whose opinion Leah has always trusted, really likes
him. The two of them are no longer just couple friends but real
friends.

Finally, Toby opens the door with Harper in his arms. The
baby is screaming and red in the face and Leah automatically
reaches out for her. 'Sorry,' Toby mumbles. 'She just won't stop
and Katelyn is in the shower and I just...' He hands Harper to
Leah and takes the Thai food bag from her.

'Don't worry, don't worry,' coos Leah and she bounces
Harper the way she has seen every mother holding a baby do.
Perhaps because her voice is calm and her smell new, Harper
stops wailing to study her with Katelyn's green eyes.

'God,' groans Toby. 'I thought she would never stop.
Katelyn has been in the bathroom for ages. Let me go and check
on her.' He looks exhausted with bloodshot eyes and messy hair,
a stain on the front of his shirt.

'Leave her, let her have a break,' says Leah and Toby smiles
gratefully. 'Has she been fed and changed?'

'She has, yeah, and she's probably due for a nap but she
won't stop crying and I'm not sure what to do... although' – he
comes over to stand next to Leah – 'look at that, you're a wizard

at this. Her eyes are closing,' he whispers. 'Maybe if we put her down, she'll sleep for a bit.'

'I don't mind holding her,' says Leah, because she feels like she could hold onto Harper all day long. She has never imagined that she would feel like this about a baby and it's not even her baby. From the moment she first held Harper, the day after she was born, Leah has been in love. Everything about Harper is incredible to her, from her tiny fingernails to her button nose. Leah doesn't get to visit often because of work but when she does come over, she is more than happy to spend the whole time holding the baby and she is also aware each time she comes over that Katelyn is struggling. She relies on Maureen, Toby's mother, a lot for help but Maureen and Ted have just left for a world cruise and will be gone for two months and Leah is not sure how Katelyn is going to manage.

'I'll hold her and you guys get some drinks,' whispers Leah as she moves towards the sofa and Toby scrambles to push a pile of washing to the side. She lowers herself slowly so that Harper stays asleep and settles back against the soft leather cushions, sighing at the perfection of the three-month- old baby.

Toby and Aaron head to the kitchen, already talking about the World Cup, the relief in Toby's voice obvious.

'You got her to sleep,' hears Leah after a few minutes and Katelyn is standing at the entrance to the living room, her hair wet and her eyes hollow with lack of sleep. She is dressed in a grubby tracksuit that bags and billows around her. New mothers complain about not being able to lose the weight they have gained while pregnant but that has not been a problem for Katelyn. Instead, she seems to have shrunk a little more each time Leah sees her.

When Harper was born, Katelyn hadn't been able to stop crying at the miracle of her baby being alive and in the world.

'Can you believe the midwife told Toby to be on the lookout for signs of postnatal depression?' Katelyn asked Leah three days after the birth as they talked on the phone. 'I can't believe how happy I am. I just want to look at her.'

Leah had laughed appreciatively at the words but she had also noted the slightly manic quality to Katelyn's voice.

'Are you getting some sleep?' she asked her.

'Oh, who needs sleep when this delicious baby is in the world,' Katelyn giggled.

Three months on and it seems that not only is Katelyn not sleeping, she's not eating either.

'How are you?' Leah asks quietly.

Katelyn shakes her head at the question. She knows how she's supposed to answer it but that's not the answer she has. 'I'm good,' she tells Leah, an answer that both of them know is a lie. What Katelyn would like to say is that she is in hell, literal hell, that she finally understands why sleep deprivation is used to torture people. Harper takes cat naps all day long and all night long. The longest the baby has slept is four hours and she only did that once. And Katelyn is slowly losing her grip on reality. Sometimes she puts the baby down to sleep and stands over her, just waiting for her to wake, knowing that if she relaxes even a little, the baby will instantly open her eyes.

'Let's get a nanny,' Toby told her yesterday, but she doesn't want a nanny. She should be able to do this. She longed for this baby for years and she should be able to be a mother. All through her childhood she had vowed to be a better mother than the one she had and now she has the chance and she is failing.

Before Maureen and Ted left for their trip, Maureen would pop over every day for a couple of hours but Katelyn could see that it was too much to ask her to be there all the time. Maureen has her own life with her friends and her work. Her job in the psychology practice she works for is flexible because a lot of her patient meetings are over Zoom, but she still has to be present mentally for them, not distracted by a baby.

Teresa calls often as well, offering help but Katelyn is conscious that she is not Harper's grandmother and she feels guilty asking for too much from her. The more help she is offered, the worse she feels, the more incapable she feels.

Katelyn has never felt the need for a mother of her own so intensely. No matter how much she reads, how much she googles, she can't seem to get the baby into a routine and behaving the way babies are supposed to. The books say one thing and Maureen another and Teresa has her opinions and the only thing Katelyn knows for sure is that she can't trust her own instincts.

She sinks onto a recliner, revelling in the freedom of not having the baby strapped to her body. When Toby is at work, she has taken to wearing the baby all day, hating the feeling of being constantly weighed down, and when Toby walks through the door at 6 p.m. she immediately hands her to him and goes for a shower, where she stands under the hot water for as long as she can possibly bear just to be alone. This is not how she was supposed to feel.

'How are you really?' asks Leah and Katelyn shrugs.

'I'm fine, just a little sleep deprived but... she's just beautiful, isn't she?' Even to her own ears the words sound forced. What she would like to say to Leah is, 'I can't believe this is my life now. I can't believe this is what I wanted. I think that I hate my baby and I'm absolutely sure she hates me.'

'You can tell me the truth, Kate, it's me,' says Leah lightly, her gaze focused on the sleeping baby. Katelyn contemplates doing just that, saying everything she wants to say instead of holding back, but there is no way she would say anything. At the back of her mind is a looming terror that someone will discover what a terrible mother she is and take the baby away, that Toby will take the baby and leave and she will be alone again just as she was when she was a child. She has to be a good mother; she has to be the best mother so that she has a family. The most terrible thing of all is that she feels like she finally understands her mother, her mother's apathy towards her, and she hates herself for that understanding.

Toby and Aaron have remained in the kitchen and Katelyn is grateful for that. She's a mess and while she cannot find the energy to care what she looks like, she always feels like Aaron is comparing her to the perfection that is Leah, whose long blonde hair is done in a neat chignon for work and whose body is perfectly encased in a tight black pantsuit. At thirty-three, Leah looks better today than she ever has. In school, Katelyn won every academic prize and Katelyn was head prefect and Katelyn was the one that everyone thought would achieve greatness, but here she is, in a stained tracksuit with breasts that are beginning to leak, an absolute failure of a human being. But Leah is a shining star, married to a gorgeous man and killing it in the business world. Jealousy is a bitter taste in Katelyn's mouth.

'Should I try and put her in her bassinet?' asks Leah, standing slowly, and Katelyn shrugs again.

'She'll probably just wake up. She usually does.'

'I'll try anyway and then maybe you and I can go for a bit of a walk, leave the boys in charge. Have you been out today?'

Katelyn's laugh is hollow with despair. 'I haven't even brushed my teeth today, Leah.'

'Okay, get your coat, it's cold outside.'

'It's after eight on a Friday night, Leah, we're not going for a walk and it's not just cold it's freezing.'

'Get your coat,' says Leah firmly, walking out, and Katelyn sits for a moment, her body relaxing now that the baby is out of the room and still quiet. Her eyes start to shut but her body jerks her awake immediately. There is no point in trying to sleep. Harper seems to know when she's asleep, almost like she can smell it, and will instantly be awake and all Katelyn wants is an hour of quiet time. She stands and goes to the front door where her coat is hanging on a hook.

'Come on,' says Leah. 'I've told them we'll be back in fifteen. It will be good for them to be in charge.'

The air outside is a shock to Katelyn's system, the cold wind hitting her in the face, forcing her to take a deep breath.

'Look,' says Leah as they begin to walk, 'I know that Toby has already suggested this...'

'What?' shouts Katelyn, fury rising up inside her. She knows what Leah is going to say and she doesn't want to hear it. She doesn't need help from a doctor. She doesn't need medicine. She doesn't need a nanny. She just needs some sleep. But that's not what makes her furious. What angers her is that Toby and Leah have been discussing her, have been discussing 'poor, not coping Katelyn'. She wants to scream with frustration. Everyone is just filled with advice for how she can get this right, even people in the supermarket stop her as she wanders around, trying to remember what to buy. *You should have that baby in a stroller.*

Ah, isn't she lovely – you'll never sleep again.

My daughter tried this wonderful mothercraft nurse and all of hers slept through the night at six weeks.

The comments drive Katelyn mad and she wants to shout at everyone who speaks to her but she's too tired to shout, so she just nods her head meekly and smiles.

———

'Now you just listen to me,' says Leah, stopping and turning to face her friend. 'You need help, Katelyn. I know you don't want to hear that. I know you've coped with every single thing that came your way but maybe this is not something you can manage your way out of. You need help. I'm your best friend and I'm telling you that you need to see someone.' Leah raises her voice, not just so she can be heard above the cold wind, but also so that she can shout some sense into Katelyn. Katelyn is not alone. She has family and friends, people who want to help her, and everyone can see that she needs a doctor and some intervention, or she won't survive this time in her child's life.

'Are you?' asks Katelyn.

'Am I what?'

'My best friend?'

'What a stupid question, of course I am,' says Leah, shocked at Katelyn's words.

'Really,' sneers Katelyn, her stomach burning with fury, 'because I know you love Harper and whenever you come over you love to hold her, but it seems to me that your life with the lovely Aaron has become so important, so filled with exciting things that I'm the last person you think of. You're off travelling and working and going out to dinner and every now and again you give me a call and say, "How's it going, Katelyn," and then you go back to your perfect life.' Katelyn feels her throat burn as she raises her voice, feels her eyes fill with tears. It feels so good to shout at someone, to shout at all, when she has spent the last three months trying to be quiet, to be silent so that the baby, the bloody baby she thought she wanted, will sleep.

'Katelyn, stop,' yells Leah. 'Just stop. You're in trouble. You need help and once you get it, you'll see that what's happening to you, your feelings, the things you're struggling with, are not things you can figure out on your own. You need help and everyone sometimes needs help.'

'Don't you sound so clever, Leah, so goddamn clever. You've got it all together, haven't you? You've definitely shown everyone who the smart one in this friendship is. You have it all.

Well done, Leah Randall – you finally have it all and I have nothing but this disgusting body and a child who hates me.'

Katelyn knows on some level that nothing she's saying is true but she hasn't been able to stop the words hitting the air, her white breath throwing them out so that everything she wants to say has finally been said.

'You're... you're not well,' says Leah. 'You're not well,' and she turns around and runs back to the house, leaving Katelyn in the street, tears streaming down her face with the knowledge that this is the last time she will see her best friend.

Swinging her arms, she walks around the block in a furious temper. She is angry with herself for shouting at Leah and angry with Leah for telling her she needs help, angry with Harper for not sleeping and Toby for leaving for work every day and Maureen for being kind and every person who has ever tried to give her advice. She hates them all and she just wants to be gone from here, just wants to be left alone. At night when she is rocking the baby in her arms, she fantasises about a one-bedroom apartment and living on her own with no one to take care of but herself. She doesn't want to be married and she doesn't want to be a mother. She doesn't want to be.

Katelyn stops walking at this thought. Really? She doesn't want to be?

At her last appointment with the nurse at the baby clinic, she and the bubbly red-headed nurse had discussed how she was feeling. Katelyn repeated, 'Fine,' to every question the nurse asked but the woman kept probing until finally she said, 'Do you ever have thoughts about hurting yourself or the baby?'

'Of course not,' Katelyn had replied, incensed. But now she wonders about that answer. She doesn't want to hurt Harper but she does long for silence and quiet and she has thought that it would be easier for everyone, Harper included, if she just isn't here. Are these the kinds of thoughts the nurse was talking about?

Katelyn looks around her, seeking out her house, but she has walked too far. Above her, the moon is hidden by clouds and a rumble of thunder in the distance warns of a winter storm.

She walks quickly back home where the lights in the front living room are on and the front door slightly open. She expects that Leah and Aaron will have left but when she gets inside, shedding her coat in the warm air, they are sitting at the table with Toby, all of them eating the Thai food Leah bought and chatting quietly. There is a place laid for her.

Without saying anything she sits down and Toby passes her a plate. 'The pad thai is really good,' he says. 'Just like you like it.'

'The baby...' she starts to say.

'Is sleeping and I'm on duty tonight. There are bottles in the fridge. Eat and then sleep, Kate, and we can figure this out in the morning.'

Katelyn doesn't look at Leah, unable to face her.

'It'll be okay,' Leah says softly.

'Yes,' Katelyn agrees, and, breathing in the lovely silence, she takes a mouthful of the pad thai, crunching on the peanuts and quickly swallowing. She's starving.

Leah watches her friend eat, her own appetite disappearing. Katelyn has no idea how lucky she is. Leah has no doubt that she's struggling but Toby loves Katelyn so completely, he will do anything he can to make sure she gets better. Leah has a feeling that if she were in Katelyn's situation, Aaron would not be as kind or understanding. He doesn't want children and she thought she would be fine without them, but she won't be and she has no idea how she's going to make her dream of a child come true.

'I think I need to see someone,' Katelyn says after her second bite of food, 'but I don't know how...'

'I'll take a week off work,' says Leah. 'More, if I have to. I'll be here so you can do what you need to do.'

'I can't ask you...' begins Katelyn, obviously ashamed that her friend is making such a generous offer.

'You didn't ask, I offered,' says Leah, sitting up straighter and making sure to not look at Aaron who she knows will hate her doing this. He's already told her that he thinks she's too involved with Katelyn's life.

'You're amazing,' says Toby to her and she gazes at him, adoring the way he looks at her with such admiration.

'I can move in here for a bit,' she says.

'You're the best,' says Katelyn, but she doesn't look at Leah when she says it. Leah doesn't let that upset her. Katelyn is not well and will get better.

Leah just keeps looking at Toby, who is so grateful for her help.

Aaron picks up his beer and takes a long swallow. 'Leah is truly amazing,' he says, but she can hear the sneering sarcasm in the words. Tonight, when they go home, she will ride in a silent car and if she presses him on what's wrong, he will attack.

Leah wishes she could just stay here tonight, just stay over and help Toby with the baby while Katelyn sleeps. She picks up her wine, allowing a rosy image of her and Toby on the sofa with the baby between them to comfort her.

'Thank you, sweetheart,' she says to Aaron, making sure that not a trace of the dislike she feels for her husband right now is present in her tone.

'Amazing,' mumbles Katelyn through a mouthful of food, but she is looking down at her plate when she says it so Leah is not sure who she's talking to.

NINETEEN

KATELYN

Tuesday Night – Three Days After the Party

If she had to use one word to describe the way she and Toby are behaving it would be 'carefully'. If she had to use one word to describe the way she feels, it would be 'dazed'.

When Toby came home from work, he called, 'Hello, my lovely girls,' as he always did, but something about him was different, removed. And something about her is more than just different. She is in shock. And so, the two of them are being careful with each other. It was easy when Harper was sitting at the table because she is always the focus of their attention, but now she is watching her half an hour of television before bed and it is just Toby and Katelyn at the dinner table and a vast space between them filled with secrets and blank spaces.

Aaron's words in the café circle in her head and her brain cannot make sense of them. Every time she has passed a mirror over the course of the afternoon she has looked into it, searching her eyes, touching her skin, wondering if she is the kind of woman who could cheat on her husband and cheat with her best friend's ex-husband. She cannot remember the party but she can remember everything before that and even though, over the course of their lunches as they discussed the idea of the gallery, Katelyn understood what it was about Aaron that made him such a compelling man, she knows that she never, ever considered the idea of sex with him, not even as a fantasy.

Had it been revenge? Had she found out before the party that Toby and Leah were sleeping together and freaked out, blanked and done something she would never do?

'Can you pass the salt, please?' Toby asks politely and she smiles at him as she does, the movement on her face feeling false.

'This is good,' says Toby, taking another bite of his roast potato.

'Thanks, I'm sure your mum gave me the recipe when we first got married.' The only thing she had been able to think of to do when she got home with Harper after preschool pick-up was to cook, to make something for her husband that she knew he would like, the husband she had cheated on, the husband who had cheated on her. It was ludicrous.

'Probably, it tastes familiar,' says Toby and Katelyn nods, wishing that she could have a glass of wine because she would give anything to numb her brain to the obvious tension between the two of them. But she's terrified to drink.

Harper had been delighted to see her after school, filled with a thousand things she absolutely had to share with her like, 'Granny Maureen put my banana in my yoghurt and I like it next to my yoghurt. And Granny Maureen read me a story from an old book called *Stories for Girls* and the girl in it didn't even have an iPad because it was sooo old and I helped Grandpa Ted find his glasses a million times and Beth sat next to me at lunch and she had popcorn chips and I want popcorn chips and Granny Maureen said your head was sore and is it better now?'

Katelyn had answered all her daughter's questions, smiling as one followed the other without Harper even listening.

Driving her daughter home from school made her tense as she concentrated hard, making sure to look in her rear-view mirror over and over again, behaving like she had when she first got her licence many years ago. Her connection to reality felt tenuous, as though it might disappear at any moment along with her memory, even though she had been assured that this would not be the case. The black hole of the party and the Sunday after looms over everything.

Her confidence returned a little as she and Harper spent the afternoon together, drawing and building a Lego city, and then when she went to the fridge to gather the ingredients for dinner, her hands moved in a way that was familiar, automatically finding tomatoes for the salad and rubbing herbs across the chicken breast. The TGA episode was over, it had to be.

Running through her mind the whole time were the things Aaron had said, his anger at her not remembering, his disbelief. *We had sex, we had sex, we had sex.* She found herself whispering the phrase over and over, until the words stopped making sense.

He had to be lying. It wasn't possible. She was not the kind of person to cheat on her husband and certainly not the kind of person to do something so reckless at her party in her own house. The more she thinks about this, the more certain she becomes. Aaron must be lying. She would never jeopardise her whole life by having sex with another man in her own home, and at a party as well. Anyone could have walked in and caught them. Did someone catch them? She shakes away the thought. It's just not something she would have done.

She left Aaron at the café with the words, 'I wouldn't have done that. You're lying,' before getting up and then running to her car, needing to get away as fast as possible, her heart heavy in her chest with disbelief and sadness.

'A couple came in today to see Marcia together,' says Toby, pulling her from her terrible thoughts.

'That's unusual.' Katelyn is having trouble swallowing. Something about the chicken is making her feel sick as she cuts into the thick white meat.

'Yeah, but it seems that they were looking for a kind of... insurance policy.'

Katelyn gives up her fight with her chicken and drops her knife and fork onto her plate, lifting her mineral water to sip instead. 'I don't understand,' she says, looking at Toby who is cutting his own piece of chicken into smaller pieces before eating it as though he's not really hungry at all.

'Well.' Toby swallows and then lifts his glass of wine to take a drink. 'He cheated on her, only once but he did, and she wanted something in place if he did it again. She wanted to know what her options were and she wanted him there to hear what would happen if they did get divorced.'

'That seems like a waste of Marcia's time. They should have gone to a therapist or an accountant or someone else.' Katelyn's hand trembles as she puts the glass down.

Toby finishes his wine and pours more into his glass, the slightly vinegary smell of the Chardonnay making Katelyn's stomach churn. She might never drink again.

'Probably, I mean she billed them, but apparently he didn't want to go to therapy... I don't know. It was a whole thing but Marcia said they both seemed to want to save their marriage.'

Katelyn folds her arms. 'If they had kids, maybe that's for the best. I mean I think there are some times when cheating, like a single incident of cheating, can be forgiven. Don't you? I mean, one incident could be seen as almost a touch of insanity, don't you think?' She asks the question quietly, controlling her voice and feeling her eyes grow hot but she can't cry. Would Toby forgive her if he knew? Does he know?

Toby finishes another glass of wine. 'Maybe,' he says, measured and slow, 'but maybe not.' He meets her gaze and Katelyn leans forward to grab the bottle of mineral water so she doesn't have to look at him. Does he know? Should she say something? If it comes out what will happen to her and to Harper?

'I'll do bath and bedtime,' says Toby now and Katelyn realises she has been staring into space, still clutching the bottle of mineral water that she puts down with a sigh.

'Yes, that would be good, thanks,' she says, looking at her husband.

He stands up from the dining room table, his plate in his hand, and she can almost see the questions circling in his head. She hopes they are just questions about her memory.

'I'm fine,' she tells him. 'I know it's Tuesday night and I know it's just after 7 p.m. and I made roast chicken for dinner. I haven't lost my memory again. I'm fine.'

'No, I didn't...' he begins.

'It's fine, Toby. I understand you're worried.' She shakes her head.

Toby nods and leaves the table. A moment later she hears him calling Harper for 'bath time and story time,' and she listens as her daughter replies.

'Yay, Daddy, I want candy bubbles, candy bubbles.'

Once he has taken Harper upstairs, she starts her clean up, gratified that she can have some time alone. After a childhood where she was mostly lonely, even with her mother in the room, Katelyn would never have expected to crave this kind of time, but Harper's early months have scarred her forever. Every night when she gets into bed, she still has to calm her body into believing that she will not be woken by a crying baby, despite it being years since Harper woke her at night. Even before she started discussing the gallery with Aaron there was a running commentary in her own head about how ungrateful she was. She had everything she had ever wanted and yet she couldn't be happy. Something was wrong with her. But she was not a morally reprehensible person, she was sure of that. 'I didn't cheat,' she whispers as she carries the untouched bowl of green salad back to the kitchen.

With her phone lying on the kitchen bench next to her, she scrapes plates and loads the dishwasher and then puts the mostly uneaten roast chicken into a bowl to go into the fridge. When her phone pings with a text, she assumes it's yet another person thanking her for the party and wants to ignore it, but then she picks it up anyway.

You don't get to pretend it never happened.

Her hand squeezes the phone as her heart races. She deletes the text and takes a deep breath to try and calm down. Surely her reaction to his news this afternoon was enough for him to understand that she wanted to forget it had happened, if it happened at all? Why would he try to make her remember? What does he gain? Why would he lie about it happening? Katelyn taps the side of her head a few times, each tap getting harder until she winces. Why can't she remember? Why can't she get her brain to remember? It is a hideous thing to have people tell you what you did, tell you how you behaved and, seemingly by extension, tell you who you are.

Putting the phone back on the bench, she returns to her cleaning, her hands moving quickly as her fears run through her mind. She is almost done when another text comes in.

Leah knows. Ask her.

I'll get her to call you right now.

You need to respond to me or I'm calling Toby. We need to talk about this. You told me you loved me.

Katelyn takes the phone into the guest bathroom, locking

the door and sitting on the cold marble-tiled floor. Her face is hot and she struggles to breathe properly. There is a pain in her chest and she wonders what a heart attack feels like.

She said she loved him? That sounds ridiculous. She would never have said such a thing. She doesn't love him. She was grateful to him for seeing her as more than just a wife and a mother, grateful to him for wanting to help her have a life for herself, but love? She loves Toby and Harper, that's who she loves.

Don't you want to know what else you said, what else you told me?

Katelyn cannot think straight. Her heart thuds, and her mouth is dry and she can feel her world imploding. What else did she tell him? Who was the Katelyn at the party and how can she and the Katelyn in the bathroom now be the same person? She wants to know what she said but she cannot have a conversation with him. Something about talking to him feels not just wrong but dangerous as well, as though by acknowledging what he has said to her, her whole life is in jeopardy – because it is.

Nausea overwhelms her and she covers her mouth as she stands, dashing for the toilet where she throws up, her body sweating and her stomach heaving.

When she's done, she sits next to the toilet, her arms wrapped around her knees. The doctor told her some nausea would be possible in the next few days but Katelyn thinks this may be more than that. This is fear and shame. This is her mistake trying to leave her body.

Her mobile phone pings with a text from Leah that Katelyn is almost afraid to read in case she and Aaron have spoken and Leah wants a confrontation, which is what she deserves if what Aaron said is true. Why had she come with her to the hospital and been so kind if she knew what had happened between

Katelyn and Aaron? Was she just waiting for Katelyn to get better to confront her? In one night, she has probably blown up her whole life. But it's not like she can hide in the bathroom or hide from what happened. She needs to accept the consequences.

With trembling hands, she opens the text.

Help. Water all over my apartment floor, pipe is broken and I can't get a plumber. Can you ask Toby to come over and fix it?

Katelyn finds herself laughing with guilty relief and then giving into tears because she cannot believe that last week she was just a stay-at-home mother who was looking forward to finally using her degree for something she was passionate about and now... now she is here. Maybe Aaron is lying when he says that Leah knows and she can just pretend none of this ever happened. Maybe this is all a ruse to get her to meet him. She always imagined that he was judging her when he looked at her, but maybe he liked her more than just as a prospective partner in a gallery. Can she just ignore him and, if Toby says something, dismiss Aaron's words? It can become a case of he said/she said. How does she do this? How can she make this go away? For a brief moment she wishes she could lose her memory of today, that today could be the missing day.

'Kate.' Toby knocks at the bathroom door.

Standing, she opens the door to find Toby outside. 'Are you okay?' he asks softly.

Katelyn nods. 'It was just... they said I might feel nauseous. What's that?' she asks.

Toby is holding a striped box with a pink ribbon in his hand.

'Oh yeah, weirdest thing, it was behind the coffee machine. I have no idea why someone would leave it there but...' He hands the box to Katelyn.

'Harper and I opened some of them this afternoon before

she got bored with all the candles and hand cream,' says Kate-lyn, her hands trembling as she opens the box. It's pink and white striped but a different shape to the underwear and still she is worried. She fumbles with the ribbon and opens the box, finding some shower gel and body cream and a card from Abigail: *Just for you, beautiful mama. Happy Birthday*.

'From Abigail,' she says and Toby nods his head, disin-terested.

'I've just had a text from Leah,' says Katelyn. 'She says a pipe is broken in her apartment and she can't get hold of a plumber and she needs you to come over and fix it. Can you go?'

'There must be a hundred plumbers she can call,' snaps Toby, his instant anger so unlike him that Katelyn steps back.

'Sorry,' he says, shaking his head.

Katelyn touches his shoulder. 'I know you're tired and it's been a long few days, but all you have to do is a quick fix and she'll get someone tomorrow. Please, she was so good about Saturday night and coming to the hospital.'

Toby has gotten used to helping Leah with things in her apartment. He's handy and likes to fix things in their own house. Leah's rental was built in the eighties and she's impatient about waiting for her building manager to fix things. Toby has been happily going over for a few months, helping her to feel less alone because she doesn't want to bother her father.

Katelyn sees Toby and Leah hugging again. Has Toby just been fixing things? Is the underwear under the bed for Leah? Why would Toby hide it there? She mentally shoves away the thoughts. She doesn't remember sex with Aaron but she does remember seeing Toby and Leah hugging? None of it makes sense. The urge to hit the side of her head again forces her to clench her fists.

'Fine.' Toby sighs, perhaps mistaking her silence for anger at his refusal to help Leah. 'I've finished reading to Harper but she wants a goodnight hug from you.'

'Of course. Maybe I'll read her something as well. We'll have a lovely time, just the two of us. I feel fine now.'

'Good, okay,' says Toby. 'Good. I'll go help her.' But there is something in the way he says the words that makes Katelyn wonder if Toby and Leah have had some kind of fight.

He's on his way she texts Leah and receives a thumbs up and a smile emoji just like she usually would, but something still feels off. What does Leah know? What does Toby know?

When he leaves, she puts it out of her mind, making sure to concentrate as she reads Harper another chapter from *The Magic Faraway Tree*, feeling comforted by the words she read to herself when she was an older child and knowing how lucky she is to be able to read to her own daughter, to give her daughter the kind of childhood she never had. Why would she have jeopardised that? Her dissatisfaction is not uncommon among mothers of small children, but no one just has sex with a friend at a party. Why on earth would she have done something like that?

'And now it's definitely time for bed, little one,' says Katelyn.

'I'm sleepy,' Harper yawns.

'Good, snuggle down now,' says Katelyn, getting off the bed.

'You lie with me, Mum, you lie here,' says Harper, her voice tight with anxiety and Katelyn realises that the last couple of days have been hard for Harper as well. She loves her grandmother but, like all children, she likes her routine and the certainty of every day. It's that certainty, that routine, that has been driving Katelyn crazy. She is suddenly hit by a wave of sadness as the possibility of the gallery disappears. There's no way she could work with Aaron now, no way she can even see him again. Will he tell Toby? It would mean the end of his friendship with Toby, she's sure of that. Maybe he will want to protect that. Maybe she doesn't need Aaron's help to find work in the art world, maybe she can begin looking for something herself, even if it's just volunteer work to start with. She needs to be here with Harper until the little girl starts school anyway. She wants to be here with her.

She lies down on the bed next to her daughter, holding her hand and breathing in her clean, sweet smell.

How could she have been dissatisfied with this? How can she be?

TWENTY

LEAH

Tuesday Night – Three Days After the Party

It was a desperate and sad move but Leah couldn't think of any other way to get Toby over here. The fact that Katelyn got him to come means that they have not had a conversation about what really happened at the party. But, of course, they wouldn't have. Toby wants to forget. But it also means they have not had the conversation about what she did today. Toby's need to sweep everything under the carpet has worked to Leah's advantage right now.

Toby's anger was frightening and she doesn't want to feel that again. It was an overreaction and she's sure he knows that. This will give him a chance to apologise and the fact that he hasn't said he won't come must mean something. She was going to text him but knew he would probably not look at a text from her. Texting Katelyn was the right way to go.

If she has him here alone, perhaps they can talk. She can apologise about coming to his office today – that was a stupid move. Not as stupid as bringing up what happened when Harper was a baby but Toby can't just continue on his merry way, forgetting everything that doesn't sit well with him. Time to lift the rug and see all the dirt under there.

Leah is not willing to let the idea of Toby go, not just yet, and all she needs is some time with him and she's sure they can figure it out.

As she fixes her make-up while she waits for Toby to come, she admires herself in her mirror. Despite everything that has happened in her life, she still looks like she did three years ago when Harper was a baby, when Harper was only three months old and Katelyn and Toby were struggling.

Leah had volunteered to stay with Toby while Katelyn got the help she needed and that had been the plan, until Maureen cut short her trip and returned home to help. She was with Harper and Katelyn during the day, until Toby came home at night when he took over. Teresa offered to go with Katelyn to her appointments so that she could listen to the doctor as well, as he prescribed medication and made suggestions. It seemed that everyone had a part to play in helping Katelyn recover except Leah. She felt more locked out of Katelyn's life than ever.

But then one afternoon, suddenly, she was needed – even if no one asked for her help.

'Maureen is seeing a patient and I have an appointment with my psychiatrist. Toby is taking time off work,' Katelyn told her on the phone.

'I could have done it. You know I love taking care of Harper.'

'It's fine, he's fine,' Katelyn said, her voice flat. Katelyn was getting better, was sleeping more, but she was still distant, almost cold as she worked with her psychiatrist to get back on an even keel.

'You should use that massage voucher I gave you for your birthday afterwards,' Leah said. 'Take some real time for yourself.'

'That's the best idea I've ever heard,' Katelyn said, a spark of lightness returning to her voice at the idea of the treat. 'I'll book right now. Toby will be fine.'

I'll come and keep you company while you babysit, Leah messaged Toby when she knew Katelyn was gone.

I'm fine.

I'll bring lunch. We can eat and you can nap.

You don't have to.

I really want to. I miss that little munchkin.

He replied with a smile emoji and Leah knew she had made the right decision to take time off work. There was no need to mention the visit to Aaron. They rarely talked during the work day. Afterwards she was deeply grateful that she had kept the visit to herself.

It began innocently enough and even as Leah thinks about this, she wonders how what happened between Aaron and Katelyn began. Was it just a drunken mistake or was it planned? Had they been seeing each other for some time, or was the night of the party the first time?

With her and Toby, she knows that the only intention she arrived with that afternoon three years ago, was to help a friend.

She bought beautifully made baguette BLT sandwiches from a place near her office and she had enjoyed the look of gratitude on Toby's face when he opened the door with Harper in one arm, his body moving up and down as he tried to get the baby off to sleep.

'Let me take her,' she said, putting the bag with the sandwiches down in the kitchen.

'Thanks,' Toby said, 'you're a lifesaver.'

Leah was practised at getting Harper to sleep and it only took her ten minutes before the baby was peaceful in her bassinet, the sheet tightly tucked around her little body so she felt secure.

Back in the kitchen Toby was wolfing down the last of his sandwich.

'Thanks so much, I was absolutely starving. I rushed out without breakfast so I could get work done before I needed to come home and then I kind of got caught up until it was time to leave. Katelyn was out the door the minute I got home and my little princess has been fussy and cranky for an hour.'

'It's fine,' laughed Leah. 'Have mine as well, I'm not that hungry.'

'No, I'm good,' said Toby with a smile, getting himself a beer, but he eyed Leah's sandwich hungrily so she stood up and got a plate, cutting the sandwich in two and giving him half.

'Beer?' he asked and she shook her head.

'A glass of wine, if you have something open.'

'Always,' said Toby, grabbing a bottle of white wine from the fridge and pouring Leah a glass.

'How are you doing?' she asked him as they shared a piece of cheesecake afterwards.

'Good,' he replied. 'Katelyn's doing well and things are getting better every day. She seems to be lighter, you know.'

'I know how Katelyn's doing, Toby. I asked how you are,' said Leah, putting a piece of the cake in her mouth, savouring the lemony sweetness.

'I'm...' Toby put his fork down and went to the fridge for another beer. 'I'm barely coping some days,' he said, opening the beer and taking a long swallow. 'She's just so... I mean, you know how she is but she needs so much from me right now. We have the same discussions over and over again and I have to keep reassuring her every time she does something, and it feels like I'm her carer and not her husband...' He stopped speaking.

'Shit, sorry, I shouldn't be saying this. She's trying to get better, she is.'

'Toby,' Leah said, leaning forward and touching him on the arm. 'You have every right to feel like this is too much. It is too much. It will get better, but right now it's really hard.'

'You're a good friend, you know,' said Toby with a smile. 'To both of us.'

Leah returned his smile, tousled his already messy curls. 'I love you both, you know.'

'I know,' said Toby, his voice husky with emotion.

'Oh, babe,' said Leah, touching him on the arm and using a term she had only used when they were dating.

And then Toby was leaning towards her and in a second they were kissing and then they were in the living room on the plush blue carpet having sex and Leah had imagined that it would feel sordid but it didn't. It felt right and natural and was as good as she remembered.

Afterwards Toby had been ashamed, had wanted her to leave as soon as possible, but only after he extracted a promise from her that she would never tell Katelyn. 'I have my own husband, Toby,' she said, beginning to feel used and disgusted with herself. 'I don't want to jeopardise my marriage over this either.'

In the car on the way back from work she cursed herself for having made such a mistake and vowed to forget it, making it home in time before Aaron to shower and throw all her clothes into the washing machine, washing away the mistake and Toby's smell on her body.

It had taken a few months of them avoiding each other without seeming to avoid each other when the couples were together, before Leah just let the incident go from her mind. But she never forgot what it felt like, how good it felt. Especially after she got divorced.

The pregnancy test in her bathroom drawer is on her mind

all the time. Her lack of a job and the fact that she is running out of money is also on her mind. But what she keeps thinking, over and over again, is that it is simply not fair. She should have had everything in life and yet here she is with nothing and Katelyn, who merely wanted to survive, has everything a person could want.

When her doorbell rings, and she opens the door, it is to find Toby, stone-faced with his shabby leather tool bag clutched in his hands. 'I don't know what you think you're playing at here,' he says, 'but I know that there's no broken pipe. I've only come over here because Katelyn asked me to. I made myself clear this afternoon.'

'There is a broken pipe,' says Leah. 'Come and see for yourself.' She leads him to her small kitchen with towels covering the floor soaking up the lightly spraying leak from under the sink. 'I tried three emergency plumbers before I texted Katelyn. I just didn't know what to do.' She wrings her hands, hoping she sounds contrite and desperate at the same time.

'Why haven't you turned off the water?' asks Toby. 'Don't you know where to turn it off?'

Leah shrugs. 'I have no idea. I looked everywhere but...' She knows where the pipe is. She's not an idiot.

'Isn't there a building manager you could call?' he asks, stepping into the kitchen, the wet towels squelching beneath his feet.

Leah feels her face grow hot as the lies pile up, one on top of the other. 'He's away,' she says. 'I tried. All I need you to do is a temporary fix of the pipe for me. It won't take more than a few minutes, I'm sure.'

Leah wonders if he can hear in her voice that she's lying, if he can hear the subterfuge. From the way he is looking at her she thinks he can. She is dressed for bed but certainly not dressed for bed alone. Instead of the usual old T-shirt and shorts, she is wearing a set of pyjamas bought for her by Aaron one Valentine's Day – short pants and a crop top covered in red hearts. A joke of a present but very comfortable and, she knows, very sexy. But Toby has barely glanced at her. She straightens her back, pushes out her chest and wets her lips, feeling a parody of a person, but she needs him to pay attention.

An hour ago, she had texted Aaron.

We need to talk.

He hadn't responded.

I don't want to talk about what happened at the party. I just want to talk about what happens now.

It took five more minutes but he finally responded to that message.

And what happens now Leah?

You like her, don't you? she replied.

And what if I do? She's not interested. I saw her today.

Really??????

Leave it Leah.

What if she tells Toby?

She won't, I'm sure of it.

But if she does?

What is it you want?

I want to make sure that everyone gets what they want.

And how does that happen?

He was interested and that was all Leah needed from him as she outlined what she wanted.

She hates Aaron, still loves him and hates him again. If he and Toby had not remained friends, she would never have had to see him again but instead of being able to move on with her life, she has seen him at dinner parties and Harper's birthday parties and barbecues.

Each time she has been invited, Katelyn has enquired tentatively, 'Toby wants to have Aaron as well but I'll tell him "no" if you don't want him here.'

Each time she has wanted and not wanted to say 'no'. If she told Katelyn not to invite him, it would mean she was not capable of seeing him because she was still hurt and not over him. But just like when Toby broke up with her, the most important thing for Leah has been to show the world that she is perfectly happy without her ex.

She and Aaron should not be together and she knows that, but that doesn't mean she should be alone.

When Leah suggested this plan, Aaron had his doubts that Toby would come over, that Katelyn would send him, but Leah was right. Katelyn will always be her best friend. And now Aaron has told her what happened at the party and even if she is questioning that, Leah knew her well enough to know that Katelyn's guilt would make her send Toby over. Katelyn will be confused and upset, wondering how she has done what Aaron says, and Leah takes some pleasure in that. Katelyn should feel bad, hideously bad. Inside Leah is cloying guilt at what she is trying to do, but somehow, she can't help herself.

On Saturday night when she caught her ex and her best friend together, she should have left. But instead, stung and horrified, she had hung around, wanting some kind of explanation, waiting for her friend to say something that would make the terrible image of the two of them in the bathroom go away.

When everyone had left, the door on the last guest closed and the house silent and chaotic, Toby had turned to his wife. 'What the hell do you think you were playing at up there? What the hell is wrong with you? How could you?'

Leah had watched the argument go round and around, waiting for her turn to confront Katelyn properly with no one around to hear her. She enjoyed watching the two of them fight. That's something she will never share with anyone. She enjoyed it.

And then Katelyn blanked. Leah should never have gone to the hospital with Katelyn and Toby, should have just left them to it, but Katelyn had seemed so vulnerable and lost that Leah was taken back to the moment they met at school at six years old. Then she had wanted to protect the sad little girl and she couldn't help wanting to do it on Saturday night, despite everything that had happened, but she's done with that now. Now she needs to look out for herself. Getting Toby here is a first step towards doing that.

'I can't stay long,' Toby says, opening the cabinet door. 'I've left Katelyn alone.'

'How is she?' asks Leah. Toby gets down on his haunches and peers at the pipe under the sink. He shrugs his shoulders. 'She'll be okay. I think we'll be okay.' Leah can't miss the word 'we'. Toby and Katelyn and Harper are a family and Leah is just an annoying woman with a broken pipe who made a mistake this afternoon. Toby opens his tool bag, takes out a wrench and begins working under the sink.

'I'm sorry about this afternoon,' says Leah. 'It was a moment of...' What should she call it? Madness? Desperation? Lust? Loneliness? 'It was just a bad moment,' she says.

'Forget it,' he says softly. Toby is a big one for just forgetting things and moving on. Leah wishes she could deal with life the same way.

'I lost my job,' she says, the words leaping from her mouth without her thinking about it. 'I lost it two weeks ago.' The words hang in the air and Leah realises this is the first time she has said it out loud. The first time she has told anyone formally. It's more final now, permanent. She's unemployed and she is divorced and alone.

She cannot help comparing herself to Katelyn once again. Katelyn, who has cheated on her husband, has conveniently forgotten what happened. Conveniently forgotten and been forgiven without ever having to face the consequences of her actions. But Leah has been dealing with nothing but consequences for years now. The consequences of allowing her friend to date a man she was in love with, and of then choosing the wrong man to marry, of losing focus at her work. It feels like her life has been one consequence after another. It is terribly unfair that Katelyn should get away with cheating on Toby, who only wants to be the best husband and father he can be.

'I'm sorry, but you'll find something else soon. You're good at what you do,' Toby says. His words are placatory, bland. He doesn't care if she finds another job or not. He doesn't care about her at all, despite how long they've been friends, despite having once been lovers, despite everything she has done for him and his family.

'Yes, I'm not worried,' she lies. 'I have a lot of interviews lined up.'

'I don't know how to fix this,' says Toby, coming back out from under the sink. 'I've got some plumber's tape. I'll wrap it around the pipe but you really need to call a plumber in the morning. There's an isolation valve under the sink to turn off the water. Maybe fill up some bottles and the kettle to get you through the night. Let me just call Katelyn and check on her.' He takes his phone out of his pocket. Leah watches as he listens to Katelyn's phone ring, sees him frown and the look of concern that crosses his face. 'Maybe she's in the shower,' he says, hanging up.

Leah fills the kettle and a couple of water bottles and Toby turns off the water and wraps the pipe.

'Can I get you a cup of tea?' she asks when he's done.

'No, I need to get home.' He takes his phone out again and calls Katelyn, something like alarm flashing across his face. 'I really need to get home.'

At the door Leah says, 'I'm sorry about everything, Toby. I know you want to just forget everything that happened and I agree. We should. Can we just put it all behind us?' He has not stayed to tea, not stayed to talk but that's okay. Plan A was that he stays here and they rekindle something, but there's also a plan B and that's where Aaron comes in.

'Yes, sure,' agrees Toby, but he sounds distracted and he turns to go down the stairs while Leah watches him. He pulls out his phone, and she hears him say, 'Listen, Mum, you're just around the corner, can you go and check on Katelyn?'

Closing the door, Leah looks at the time on her phone. By the time he gets home it will have been more than an hour.

She cannot help the smile that crosses her face. It feels good to finally be in control of something, to finally be the one making the decisions. Not her boss, not her husband, not her friend, just her. Things are going to change for the better. She can feel it.

TWENTY-ONE

KATELYN AND LEAH – THIRTY-FIVE
YEARS OLD

'Okay, now you can blow out the candles, Harper,' says Katelyn to her daughter, whose green eyes are saucer big in her two-year-old face as she studies the white-frosted chocolate cake decorated with plastic mermaids all adorned with pink and purple curved fishtails. Harper blows dramatically on the candles and everyone claps as though she has achieved a miracle.

'At least she didn't spit on it,' says Leah and Katelyn laughs.

'I'll cut it up,' says Maureen, picking up the cake to keep it away from Harper's reaching hand.

'And I will have two pieces,' says Toby.

'No, Daddy, it's my birfday,' says Harper sternly. 'I should get two pieces.'

'You're right,' agrees Toby, 'and that's exactly what you will have. You're going to need a lot of energy to help me build the doll's house from Granny and Grandpa.'

On the floor of the living room is a timber doll's house that Maureen and Ted have spent a fortune on for Harper. Its pieces slot into place and create a lovely home that Maureen and Ted have also bought furniture for. Katelyn thinks it's far too mature a present for Harper but Maureen is so excited by the idea of it that she hasn't said anything. Her mother-in-law is a godsend, always available for help and delighted to spend every moment she can with her granddaughter. Katelyn has no idea how she would have survived the last two years without her.

With plates of cake in their hands, Katelyn and Leah stand, getting ready to go outside and away from where Harper, Toby and Ted are sitting around the dining room table and Ted is telling Harper his dad jokes or, in his case, grandpa jokes. 'Why did the banana go to the doctor?' Ted asks and Harper bites down on her lip, thinking hard and then she shrugs her shoulders. 'I don't know, why?'

'Because he wasn't peeling well,' says Ted and Harper giggles as Toby laughs along with her.

Katelyn has decorated the table with a pink and purple plastic cloth where mermaids cavort under the sea surrounded by fish and shells. It's just a small party to celebrate Harper turning two. Katelyn hadn't wanted anything big. She is still conscious of how difficult the first few months after Harper was born were, of the darkness that surrounded her, of the despair she felt. It had taken a long time before she agreed to get help, but between therapy and some medication she had finally fought her way out of the mire of depression that surrounded her.

A secret that she is keeping from everyone, including herself, is that even after Harper started sleeping through the night, even after there were routines, and hours of peace and quiet she could count on, Katelyn still feels as though she has lost some part of herself. That there is a part of her that will never return. The Katelyn before, the Katelyn who so desperately wanted a baby, no longer exists and every day she struggles to come to terms with who she is now. A lot of the women in her mothers' group are either pregnant or talking about getting pregnant again. Some have even fallen naturally without having to resort to IVF again. But Katelyn cannot go through the whole thing again, not IVF, not birth and not those lost months with a new baby. Toby brings up the idea constantly, pointing out babies in carriages when they are at the park and talking about how this time it will be different. 'We'll get a nanny, we'll all be ready, it will be nice for Harper to have a sibling.' Katelyn knows that no matter how ready everyone is, she's the one who has to have the baby, feed the baby, be with the baby. And she's not going to do that.

'I think I'm getting a headache,' says Leah and Katelyn knows that even though Leah loves Harper dearly, the whole family party is a bit much for her at the moment. She takes Leah outside and together they sit on the porch swing rocking gently in the still warm autumn breeze.

'How are you?' asks Katelyn.

'You know,' Leah answers with a shrug.

'No, I don't,' says Katelyn. 'How are you doing really?' She takes a bite of the cake, wrinkling her nose at the sweetness of the frosting. Leah holds her cake in her hands, not even bothering to pretend she is eating it. She's lost a lot of weight in the last few months and Katelyn knows that she prefers the solace of alcohol over the nourishment of food right now.

She sighs. 'I'm okay but at the same time I'm not okay, not anymore. I don't even understand what happened. We were so in love one moment and then he was just... it's so hard to talk about this because I know he and Toby are still friends, but he wasn't nice. There was something about him that changed all of a sudden. He was angry, mean.'

Katelyn nods. She has heard this before and she is sure she will hear it again. Sometimes talking is the only thing that helps.

Leah knows she's not telling the whole truth, not really. There had always been something about Aaron, something simmering, something fierce inside him. When they were married, she knew there were lines she could not cross, things she shouldn't say. Despite that, she loved him. But she hadn't been able to help herself from crossing one line, from asking for something she knew he didn't want to give her. When they were dating he explained he never wanted children and she accepted that. But after Harper was born something inside Leah opened up, reached out, wanted more. She bonded with Harper in a way she had never imagined possible and because of that it became impossible to imagine a life where she would not have a child of her own. She mentally pushes away one afternoon when she came over to help and things with her and Toby got a little complicated. It's easier not to think about that. What she mostly thinks about now is having a child, or she did when she was still married. Even knowing Aaron's stance on kids, Leah began to push and the harder she pushed the worse Aaron became. His temper flared daily and his anger was always directed at her.

'The way he told you he wanted a divorce was awful,' agrees Katelyn.

'Cruel.' Leah nods, pushing her feet against the timber deck to make the porch swing move.

A terrible night two weeks before they separated returns to her and she can see Aaron with his fist clenched, waving it at her, the veins on his forehead bulging and his skin puce with anger. It had been an innocuous enough conversation to begin with, but it had been the beginning of the end for their marriage. At work one of the juniors, a woman five years younger than Leah, had returned to work to show everyone her beautiful baby. As all the female staff cooed and smiled and asked to hold the child, Leah had felt her heart a stone in her chest. She had moved away and retreated to her office and her spreadsheets. But Deborah had wanted to share her child with her old boss. After a few minutes there had been a soft knock at her glass door and Deborah was there, her baby in her arms.

'I thought you might like a hold before I go,' she said sweetly.

Leah stood up, and nodded, knowing that if she did anything but nod, if she spoke even a single word, tears would stream down her face. She opened her arms and Deborah placed the snugly wrapped little boy close to Leah's chest. Leah smelled his newborn milk smell, watched his eyelashes flutter and his little mouth purse in his sleep. She had asked Deborah to take pictures on her phone of her and the baby. Returning home that evening, she found Aaron in his study, going over the shift roster for his security guards.

'Good day?' she asked, slouching into a leather armchair next to his desk and kicking off her shoes.

He leaned back in his desk chair, stretching his arms over his head. 'Yeah, got the contract for the hotel in the city.'

'Well done.' She smiled.

'You?' he asked and she had known as she started talking what she was doing.

'Great. Look,' she said, standing up and opening the gallery on her phone, her voice high and bright. 'Deborah brought her son to show us today. Look how cute he is.' She had turned her phone to him, showing him picture after picture of the baby in her arms.

'What the hell is wrong with you?' he muttered, standing from his office chair. He left his study and walked to the kitchen, pouring himself a glug of whisky in a crystal glass. 'Who takes so many pictures of somebody else's baby?' His voice was soft with menace.

'I... just... he's just lovely, isn't he lovely?' Leah asked, knowing that with every word she was stepping closer to the line that she wasn't supposed to cross but she couldn't help herself. It had become her habit to bring up babies whenever she could, hoping that one day she would somehow change his mind and Aaron would agree to one child.

'We've had this discussion,' said Aaron, pouring himself another glug. 'We've had it over and over again. I don't want a child. I won't have a child. I know you think it would make a lovely accessory to go with your bags and your shoes, but children don't live in the cupboard when you're bored.'

'That's why you think I want a baby?' she yelled, stung by the comment and what it meant for the way he saw her.

Aaron took a sip of his whisky and sighed. 'Leah, not everyone needs to be a mother. We have a nice life. We travel and you can walk into any store you want and buy whatever you want. You don't want a baby; you want a new pair of shiny shoes.'

'You are such a bastard,' she spat.

'Then why have a baby with me?' He smirked. 'Maybe my baby will be a bastard too.'

Leah realised the conversation was going in the wrong direction. 'Maybe we should just talk about it some more,' she pleaded. 'I feel like we haven't spoken about it enough. You won't have to do anything, I promise you. I will be completely in charge. You don't understand how important this is to me.' Her nose began to run and a tear slipped down her cheek. 'I want to have a baby and if you loved me you would want to have one with me. It's what people do.'

'I'm done talking about it, Leah.'

'Well, I'm not done and I'm sick of you thinking that you get to make all the rules in this marriage,' she shouted, her despair turning into fury.

Aaron stepped towards her, his fist clenched. 'I'm not having this discussion again,' he hissed. 'Not again,' and then he shoved her so she hit her hip against the marble counter. She hadn't been able to help her tears as she heard the front door slam, knowing that he would not be back that night.

He returned the next morning and for two weeks they were polite and distant, but one night she got home from work late to find he had ordered her favourite Mexican food and laid it all out on their glass dining room table.

Hope flared inside her. Usually when he apologised for an angry outburst, he bought her flowers or a piece of jewellery and left it on her bedside table. She thought the Mexican food meant that he wanted a conversation and that meant he had reconsidered, had thought about what she said.

'This looks great,' she said, putting her briefcase down and kicking off her shoes.

'It's your favourite.' He smiled. 'I thought we could just talk.' He poured her a glass of red wine and dimmed the lights in the living room.

She sat down and took a sip of her wine. 'Delicious,' she said and then she filled her plate from the takeaway containers, putting the nachos with slow cooked beef on first and adding some salt baked chicken. 'I'm glad you want to talk,' she said. And then she took a bite of her food, enjoying the flavours as she waited for him to begin because she knew he would begin with an apology, and then they would have to have the obligatory conversation about how much stress he was under. She was fine with that as long as the conversation eventually led to a discussion about having a baby.

'I want a divorce,' he said, picking up his wine to take a sip and Leah felt a corn chip lodge in her throat. She started coughing and picked up her serviette to spit the piece of chip into it, her eyes tearing up as she gasped for breath while Aaron watched her, his blue eyes blank of emotion.

'Is that a joke?'

'No. I've been thinking a lot over the last two weeks and I realised that it's not that I don't want a kid. It's that I don't want a kid with you.' He took another sip of his wine and tucked into his own food calmly as though he had simply told her about his day.

'You can't be serious,' gasped Leah, when she was breathing normally again. Her head was spinning as though she had drunk the whole bottle of wine alone instead of just one sip from her glass. 'You can't be serious,' she repeated, hoping that this was some kind of joke, a sick joke, but a joke anyway.

Aaron finished his wine and poured himself another glass. 'Look, we're both adults here and we've only been married for three years. This doesn't need to become a big thing. I'm not happy. And I think that you need a different kind of man, a man who wants to have kids with you. You can make this easy or you can turn it into a battle, but either way, we're done. I'll give you a couple of weeks to get your stuff out.'

Beyond shocked, Leah stood up from the table, her desire to maintain her dignity kicking in. 'That's fine, Aaron. I'll leave now and come back for my stuff tomorrow.' She walked away, trying to process what had just happened, but also trying to process the feeling that was buzzing around under the anger and hurt and confusion.

She examined the feeling as she donned her high heels again and then grabbed a bag and filled it with enough clothes for a few days, all the while listening to Aaron eating his food and drinking his wine as though nothing at all had happened. At the front door to their apartment, she paused to look at him because she could see the dining room from there but he was on his phone, his eyes moving as he read something. There had never been a man who looked more unconcerned than Aaron did at that moment. Leah left the apartment, not slamming but rather closing the door softly behind her.

After a few days in a hotel, she realised what the feeling was. It was relief. She didn't want to have children with Aaron, she just wanted a child and she had never been able to picture him cradling a baby. He barely looked at Harper when they got together with Katelyn and Toby. He was self-centred and prone to anger. He was not father material. She held onto that relief when she understood that Aaron had never put her name on the deed to the apartment and that she had very little money to her name. She held onto that relief when Toby asked, so sweetly, if he could still be friends with Aaron and she agreed, but she was struggling to hold onto that relief anymore. She didn't love Aaron and perhaps she never had, but being thirty-five and back looking for dates was terrifying and soul-destroying.

'I know that this has been a really rough few months for you. I'm hoping that once the papers are signed you can be completely done with him and move on,' says Katelyn.

'Except for when I see him here,' says Leah softly.

'I can tell Toby to stop seeing him, you know he'll do it. Toby loves you.'

'It's fine,' sighs Leah, pushing the swing to make it rock again. 'It's fine. It's just this wasn't exactly the plan for my life.' She takes a tiny amount of cake and pushes it down with her fork, watching the colours mingle.

'I know it's been hard but things will get better,' says Katelyn. 'One day you'll find somebody new and it'll be okay.'

Leah nods her head as though she agrees with Katelyn. Perhaps she will find someone but perhaps not and she can feel the ticking of her biological clock loud and strong inside her.

'Let's not talk about me anymore,' she says to Katelyn. 'How are you? How are you feeling?'

Katelyn's laugh is hollow. 'You know me, being the best mum in the world,' she says.

Leah nods her head as though she understands but she doesn't, she really doesn't understand. She has been nothing but supportive of Katelyn and her struggles, but what she would really like to do is grab her oldest friend by the shoulders and shake her and shout, 'Do you understand what you have here? Do you understand how lucky you are? After everything you went through to have Harper, how can you not love every moment you have with her now? How can you not love every moment of your life every day?' But Leah says none of this and instead she takes a bite of the overly sweet cake, hoping that it will dispel some of the bitterness she feels.

'I'm trying to just be in the moment every day,' Katelyn says as though she has heard Leah's thoughts.

'You should,' says Leah. 'Harper is an angel.'

Katelyn laughs again. 'That's what everyone says and I adore her, you know I do.' She looks at Leah, making sure her friend understands that to be the truth. 'Toby wants another child.'

'You should have another,' says Leah and Katelyn can hear she's trying to be supportive.

'I don't...' she begins as she remembers overhearing Aaron and Toby talking one night when he came over to visit. As soon as he arrived, she took herself off to bed, not wanting to be near him when he had hurt her friend so badly, but knowing that he needed Toby as a friend. Upstairs she had read for a while until she remembered that she had forgotten to take bread out of the freezer for the morning and so she tiptoed down the stairs, stopping when she heard Aaron speaking.

'You don't make a family with a woman like Leah. She's too into herself,' Aaron had said. 'You make a family with a person like Katelyn.'

Mixed emotions flowed through Katelyn. She was incensed on behalf of her friend, but also understood that sometimes Leah came across like that; she was also buoyed by Aaron's description of herself because she spent a lot of time questioning her mothering. She didn't wait for Toby's reply, just ducked into the kitchen and took out the bread and then went back to her book.

'Harper would love a sibling,' Leah says quietly.

Katelyn finds herself exhausted by the idea of having to explain herself. Leah knows what she went through – it shouldn't be difficult to understand. 'It was so... hard the first time. And what if it happens again? Do you all want to watch me suffer?' she says petulantly.

'Nobody wants you to suffer, Katelyn,' says Leah, her tone slightly harsh. 'But you're so lucky to have a man who wants to be with you and who wants to have another child with you. He's been nothing but kind and supportive.'

Sometimes when Leah talks about Toby, Katelyn thinks she can hear a subtext, an undercurrent of Leah's regret that she broke up with Toby. But she would never say anything about it to Leah. There would be no point and Leah is dealing with her divorce, hurting and sad.

'Looks like neither of us are where we want to be,' says Katelyn.

'I guess,' agrees Leah, 'but at least you have Harper and Toby. What do I have?'

Katelyn had wanted a sympathetic ear, had wanted Leah to say that Toby was being ridiculous, but Leah wasn't going to give her that. Leah was worried about her own life.

'You have me,' says Katelyn, 'and I'll always be here for you.' She stands up from the porch swing. 'Come on, let's get you a glass of wine to go with the cake you're not eating.'

Leah laughs and stands up. 'Yep, that's me. Always ready for a drink.' As she follows Katelyn inside, Leah thinks that sometimes she hates her oldest friend, really hates her.

TWENTY-TWO

Tuesday Night – Three Days After the Party

When Harper falls asleep next to her, Katelyn waits until she hears the deep even breaths that mean she will not easily be disturbed, and then slides off the bed and walks slowly out of her little girl's bedroom where stars shine on the ceiling.

Katelyn is relieved to get some quiet time, relieved that Toby is helping Leah so that she can just sit on the sofa and think. She knows that it's counterproductive to try and remember her encounter with Aaron but she can't help it. No matter how hard she tries, she cannot picture the party. She thinks she remembers Leah arriving and taking a selfie with her. But now that she thinks about it, she's not even sure she remembers that. Perhaps because she has a picture on her phone, she thinks she remembers it. Perhaps her issues started before the party even began.

In the next few days, she will have to see Leah because she can't avoid her forever. For one thing, Leah has all the pictures of the party and seeing them may jog her memory. But Katelyn knows that the minute her old friend sees her, everything will be out in the open. If Leah is having an affair with Toby, she will know. If what Aaron said about the two of them and Leah knowing is true, Katelyn will know. One moment she is furious with Toby because of his possible affair with Leah and the next she is devastated over her choice to have sex with Aaron. Can she trust Aaron? Can she trust herself?

When she asked Toby to go over to Leah's apartment, she was gratified to see his irritation because maybe it meant that her assumptions were incorrect, or maybe it meant that was exactly what Leah and Toby wanted her to think.

Slumping onto the sofa in the living room, Katelyn buries her head in her hands. This is so hard because she can't trust her own brain. If she knew anything for sure she would know how to react but she doesn't and so she's terrified to make a decision or a move and find that she's been wrong all along.

After a few minutes she decides that she cannot stand her own thoughts anymore. She needs to do something else, to concentrate on something else, so she goes into the kitchen to finish cleaning up. As she cleans, tipping most of her food in the bin and smiling ruefully as she remembers doing exactly the same thing when she was pregnant with Harper, she shakes her head. Everything tasted strange and wrong when she was in her first trimester. Holding a plate that she has just scraped clean, Katelyn stands completely still. Everything tastes wrong. 'No,' she thinks. 'No.' Dropping the plate into the dishwasher she runs up the stairs to her bathroom and finds the pack of pregnancy tests that were left over from when they were trying for Harper.

They've been in the back of the drawer for four years already. When they were trying for Harper, she bought one pack after another, always hopeful, always disappointed until they began IVF and were finally successful. She had wanted to throw out the unopened packet of tests she had when she was pregnant with Harper but instead, she shoved them to the back of a bathroom drawer, keeping them there as a reminder of the many years of disappointment. And perhaps hoping that she would be able to use them again for a second child. That was until her experience with post-partum depression and her desire to only have one child.

Now she opens the drawer and scrabbles through old perfume bottles and hotel vanity packs that she has collected until she finds the box. It's been opened and one test has been used. She sits on her haunches, her head beginning to pound.

She doesn't remember doing a pregnancy test. Not since she had Harper. Actually having the baby and caring for the baby had been such a shock to her system she had been certain she could never do it again and so when her doctor suggested low-dose birth control she accepted.

When would she have taken the test? She hasn't had any scares as her period arrives with clockwork regularity.

Her stomach twists, and she thinks she's going to throw up, but then she takes a deep breath and swallows a couple of times.

It shouldn't be possible because she struggled for Harper and she's on birth control. Did she miss a pill? Has it stopped working or... she doesn't finish the thought. 'Find out first,' she instructs herself.

Pulling her pants down and sitting on the toilet, her fingers fumble as she pulls a test from the packet and struggles to open it, cursing when her pulling splits the packet and the test bounces on the floor.

'It's not possible, not possible,' she keeps muttering as she uses the test, not needing to read the instructions. She did so many of them, she could do one in her sleep.

Placing the test on the floor, she washes her hands and then sits down next to it, watching it carefully as though it may suddenly get up and run away.

Downstairs, the front doorbell chimes. It's not Toby because he comes in through the garage. She glances at her phone and sees that it's after 8 p.m. Who is ringing a doorbell at this time of night?

Before it can ring again and wake Harper, she shoves the test into the bottom drawer of the vanity unit and goes to answer it, running down the stairs.

Aaron is standing at the door and as soon as she sees him, Katelyn starts to shut it again but he jams his foot in and says, 'No way, Katelyn. You don't just get to tell me I'm lying and run off.'

'Toby's here,' she hisses. 'Just leave. I'll meet you another time.'

Aaron chuckles as he pushes against the door. 'Toby is at Leah's apartment.'

The shock of his words makes Katelyn step back and Aaron steps inside, closing the door behind him, looming over her and reminding her of just how big he is.

'Look,' she begins, 'Harper is asleep upstairs and this is obviously not the time. If you go, I can meet with you tomorrow and I won't leave this time – we can talk things through.'

She cannot begin to think about why Aaron has enlisted Leah in this and what Leah may be saying to Toby right now. She just needs this man gone, out of her house and away from her daughter.

'Yeah, I don't think that's going to happen, Katelyn.' He steps forward, his voice dropping to a whisper. 'Come on, Kate, you like me, I know you do. Saturday night was' – he runs a hand along her cheek and shakes his head – 'just something amazing,' he says, with a smile. 'We can be together, you and me. We can raise a child or children. I won't care if it's hard. All this time, I've been looking at you and thinking about what it would be like to be with you, what it would be like to come home to a woman who's cooked a meal and who's there for me no matter what.'

'Oh, please,' Katelyn says, sneering, stepping back, out of

the reach of his hands. 'Don't romanticise me for being a stay-at-home mother. You just want what you can't have, Aaron. Leah loved you and you hurt her. You need to leave now. I'm calling Toby.' Her phone is in her pocket and she takes it out, remembering she put it on silent when she was lying with Harper. She's missed a call from Toby.

'No,' says Aaron, moving quickly towards her and grabbing the phone. 'We need to talk.'

'Aaron, please,' she says, stepping back again, away from him, crossing her arms over her chest. 'Whatever happened, you have to believe that it was just a moment of madness, too much alcohol, not me.'

'That's crap,' says Aaron, his tone low, anger creeping in. 'You hadn't even been drinking, Katelyn. You told me that when you closed the bathroom door and then grabbed me. I said, "Katelyn, you're drunk and you'll regret this," and you said, "I've wanted to do this since the first time I saw you and I haven't had a single thing to drink tonight except mineral water and fruit juice."'

'Obviously I was lying,' she says, stepping further away from him as he takes another step towards her. The words don't sound like her words, the behaviour doesn't sound like her.

'You knew exactly why I followed you upstairs, sweet Katelyn. You knew the minute you took my gift and took it away to hide it. I know you must have looked at it before you hid it away. You must have and I know you understood what it meant.'

'The underwear,' gasps Katelyn. 'You gave me the underwear.'

'Please don't pretend you didn't know that I wanted you. All you ever talked about was wanting to be more than a wife and a mother. I can give you that, Katelyn. I can give you everything.'

'I meant I wanted a career, Aaron. I wanted the gallery.'

'You wanted me.'

'I don't want you. I don't care what I said on Saturday night. I don't want you and I never have. I love Toby.'

'Yeah, yeah, I don't buy that. Yes, no, yes, no. You're a bit of a tease, Kate. You like the teasing and then you say "no," but I'm not a teenage boy you can play with. I'm a man and you liked it in the end... until we got interrupted.'

'Oh my God.' Katelyn cannot breathe properly. There is not enough air in the room. 'Are you... are you saying you forced me?' How is this possible?

'No way.' His skin reddens, fury in his face. 'You wanted it, you know you did.'

'I don't remember anything,' she shrieks. 'I lost my memory. I can't remember the whole party, nothing.'

'That's so convenient, isn't it?' he sneers. 'Little Kate doesn't want to be a bad girl.'

Katelyn feels sick. She needs to get him out of her house, away from her child. 'Aaron,' she begins, lowering her tone, goosebumps of fear rising on her skin. His fists are clenched and a scowl takes over his whole face. *Keep him calm, keep him talking. Get him out of here.* 'I've lost my memory. I had to go to the hospital. Something was already going on with me on Saturday night because I can't remember the party and I don't remember being with you... I just don't and I'm sorry. If we did have sex, then you have to just accept it was a moment of madness and I never want to repeat it.'

She can't even begin to think about what it might have meant that she tried to say no, she tried to say no and he refused. What happened to her, what happened to her the night of her party?

There is danger here. She can feel it. Aaron is a bomb that needs to be defused before he goes off. *Keep him calm, keep him talking, get him out of here.* 'I'm sorry. I've behaved really badly and I hope you can forgive me. I know you and Toby are friends.' As she speaks, she takes small steps backwards, trying to figure out how close she is to the staircase. If she can run upstairs and get to her room, she can lock that door, but that would mean Harper is alone. She needs to pick up Harper and then go to her bedroom. There is no way she is fast enough for that.

Aaron snaps his fingers. 'Easy as that. You messed up and now I need to be gone so you can get back to your nice life.' He takes another step towards her and the slightly spicy scent of his aftershave turns her stomach.

'It's not like I haven't worked for this, Katelyn. What do you think all those lunches discussing the gallery were about? You didn't actually think I believed you capable of running something like that?' He laughs.

Katelyn grows hot with humiliation, her heart racing as she realises that this is the truth. 'You never wanted me to...' she begins and then she stops herself. *How could you have believed him, you're such an idiot, you're never going to be anything more than a mother and you're a shitty mother as well. You're no better than your own mother.* Her eyes close briefly as her mother's face appears in front of her, sneering and filled with disdain for her only child.

'I don't care,' she snaps, opening her eyes, not sure if she is speaking to Aaron or the spectre of her mother. 'You need to leave now,' she says firmly, struggling to keep her fear out of her voice. She needs him out of her house and placating him is not working.

'Hold on, hold on now,' he says, his tone gentle and wheedling. 'Even if you can't run it alone, I will buy the gallery for you or set you up somewhere else, I promise you that. If we're together you'll have whatever you want.' He smiles and she can see the smile is meant to be reassuring and seductive at the same time, but it's just scary. She needs him to leave.

'I'm really sorry, Aaron,' she says, her head pounding so

hard she winces. 'Please go. Toby will be back soon and it's just...' She waves her hand.

'No, no, Katelyn, it's just nothing. Come on, Katelyn, you want to be with me, you know you do.' He steps forward again, his voice just above a whisper as he repeats, 'You want to be with me, I know you want to be with me,' and then he touches her shoulders, making her flinch and step back.

Katelyn has tried saying sorry and she has tried being polite but the effort it has taken to repeatedly apologise for something she doesn't remember and something she suspects might have been forced on her, has exhausted her patience. Fury at having to do this now when she is struggling to comprehend what has happened to her mind, takes over her body. 'Look, it was a mistake,' she hisses, mindful of Harper upstairs. 'It should never have happened and I'm not even attracted to you. I may have said I wasn't drinking but that was a lie. It was an alcohol-fuelled mistake. I had so much to drink I lost my memory, for God's sake. Just get out of my house.' Her voice falters. Why is he looking at her like that? How can blue eyes suddenly seem black?

She steps back again.

Aaron leaps forward and grabs her shoulder hard and as she tries to wrench away from him, hissing, 'Aaron, stop,' he moves his hands to her neck.

'I am so sick of being lied to by women who think I'm some sort of plaything. Leah thought she could change the rules and now you think the same thing. I am so sick of being treated like an idiot, like I've misunderstood the signals.' He squeezes and pushes her back at the same time until she is standing next to the sofa in the living room and then he pushes her down, holding onto her neck so tightly she is certain that she is going to black out. Pain shoots up into her head and it feels like her eyes are bulging as her breathing grows thready with desperation.

'Please... Harper,' she rasps, but he keeps squeezing.

'I am not a joke, do you understand that, Katelyn? I am not a joke.'

Black spots appear in front of her eyes, surreal disbelief surrounds her. This cannot be happening. It cannot be happening.

As she starts to lose consciousness, she thinks that she can hear the doorbell chime but realises that the ringing is in her ears. She is going to die. She is leaving Harper and there is probably another child inside her and she is going to...

TWENTY-THREE

LEAH

Tuesday Night – Three Days After the Party

When Toby leaves, Leah glances at the time. It's just after eight thirty. In her kitchen she pours herself a large glass of wine, reasoning that just one can't hurt. There are four jobs she found this afternoon that she wants to apply for and she needs a clear head for that.

Sitting on her sofa, she clicks on the television and finds a rerun of *Friends* that she can watch mindlessly. She tries to imagine Toby arriving home and seeing Katelyn and Aaron together. Because that's what she hopes will happen. She hopes that whatever passion consumed Katelyn at her party will return and Toby will walk in to find his good friend and his wife melded together in a steamy kiss or worse.

She cannot help her smile. Some sort of weird brainstorm may have allowed Katelyn to deny what happened at the party, but her memory is fine now and she won't be able to talk her way out of things again. She takes a big mouthful of the wine to swallow down any guilt she feels at conspiring with her ex-husband. Katelyn won't experience another TGA surely? And once Toby catches Aaron and Katelyn together, then perhaps he will realise that there's no reason he and Leah can't be there for each other.

She can see him returning tonight, tears in his eyes. 'I caught them again,' he will say. 'I can't believe she did this to me. Maybe the whole memory thing was a lie but I can't be with her anymore. You're right, Leah, right about everything.' And then he will take her in his arms and they will make love and soon she will be living in a lovely house and she will wake every morning to smiles from her own child who will have brown curls like Toby and blue eyes like she does.

Lost in her daydream, she reasons that she's only thirty-five and there's still plenty of time to have a child and until then she can be a stepmother to Harper and maybe they can all become one big blended family and— Her email pings and she opens it, finding yet another rejection.

What kind of a person sends a rejection at night? She wouldn't want to work for the kind of company that does that anyway. But her daydream is shattered and her wine is finished and hopelessness begins to creep through her.

Getting off the sofa she goes to the bathroom and opens the bottom drawer of the vanity, staring down at the pregnancy test.

After a few minutes she sighs and picks it up, throws it in the garbage bin next to the vanity. She can hear Aaron's words. 'What kind of a person takes so many pictures with someone else's baby?'

The same kind of a person, she supposes, who takes someone else's positive pregnancy test and pretends to herself that it's hers. Aaron is right, she really is crazy. She just wanted it to be hers, wanted to be one of the pregnant women in the circle discussing names and cravings.

Toby will probably get home and find Katelyn alone and Toby and Katelyn will go back to their lives and wouldn't you know it – have another baby. They will be a picture-perfect family of four. All they need is a cute dog.

Back in the kitchen, Leah grabs the bottle of wine and takes it to the sofa with her. There's no point in pretending she's not going to finish it tonight and there's no point in pretending she's going to apply for any more jobs. She's sick of her life, sick of trying to make things come out the way she wants them to.

On the sofa she fills her glass to the top when her phone rings and seeing it's Toby, she answers it, a sliver of hope making her heart beat faster.

'Oh God,' moans Toby. 'Oh God, Leah, he's... she's... the police are coming, the ambulance is here, you have to come. Oh God, you have to come.'

TWENTY-FOUR

KATELYN AND LEAH – THE DAY BEFORE THE PARTY

While she unpacks groceries, she munches on some cheese and crackers, hungry even though she finished breakfast a couple of hours ago. On the counter is a list of things she needs to do before the party tomorrow night and she keeps glancing at it, making sure that there's nothing more to add. She's confirmed with the caterer, who will be dropping off food for her to warm up, and the dining room table is covered in plastic bags filled with decorations. The idea of a party was a lot more fun than the actual execution but she's sure she'll get it done. Maybe Leah will come over and help although maybe not. It feels like Leah is pulling away a little, like the divorce had not only meant that she and Aaron have parted but also that a wedge has been driven between Leah and Katelyn. Leah keeps telling her how lucky she is to have Toby and Harper, and Katelyn knows she is, but no one's life is perfect. Leah sees what she wants to see.

At the supermarket she had run into a woman she met when she was having IVF.

It was so random, she had just rounded a corner and there was Monica, standing in the condiment aisle reading the label on a bottle of tomato sauce.

'Monica,' Katelyn had exclaimed and the woman had turned, but it had taken her a moment to remember.

'Katelyn,' said Katelyn. 'We met at the IVF support group.'

'Oh yes,' said Monica, a brief smile appearing. 'How are you?' Monica had not joined the mothers' group some of the women formed after they got pregnant. She had been invited but she had never come.

'I'm good,' said Katelyn, smiling. 'How are you?' and she glanced down at Monica's swollen belly. The last time she had seen Monica was just after she got pregnant, at around the same time Katelyn got pregnant with Harper, but she hadn't wanted to ask anything in case that pregnancy had not been successful.

'Just lovely,' said Monica, stroking her belly. 'My son, Jock, just turned three and this one is a girl so we'll have our pigeon pair.'

'Congratulations,' Katelyn said, wondering why she wanted to cry. 'My Harper is three as well.'

'Any plans for another? You wouldn't believe it but this one just happened naturally. We were amazed but I'm just so grateful.' Monica's dark eyes shone with sincerity. She radiated happiness and Katelyn could see that she was completely settled in her life and loving every moment of being a mother. Without Monica having to say anything else, Katelyn felt judged for her ambivalence towards motherhood and at the same time she understood that she was projecting. Monica was just asking a question.

'Oh, I think one is enough for us,' Katelyn said, hearing the slight wobble in her voice as she trotted out the same thing she had told all the other women in her mothers' group. She feels like a traitor, like she was given the opportunity for one child and is betraying every woman who is still trying for a baby by simply not ever wanting another.

'They can be a handful,' Monica agreed and then her phone

rang and while she was answering it, Katelyn moved off, relieved to get away.

Now she stops her unpacking to think about the interaction. Monica looked so happy. Would another baby make her happy? She doesn't think so, really doesn't think so, but what if she's wrong? Right now, the thing in her life she's most excited about is the gallery with Aaron and she's determined to sit down with Toby the day after the party and talk about the discussions she's been having with Aaron. She's hopeful that Toby will be happy for her, hopeful but unsure. Toby really wants another child but perhaps he will be willing to wait. Maybe she just needs more time before committing to another child.

She is turning thirty-six tomorrow and time to have a baby is ticking away, but women have babies older and older these days. Maybe it won't be so hard next time?

She shakes her head and goes back to unpacking her groceries. 'Cold drinks,' she suddenly shouts, and she quickly sends Toby a text asking him to pick some up on the way home. The party is turning into a monster, consuming her every thought, and she keeps forgetting things.

'It doesn't have to be perfect, just fun,' Toby said last night, but Katelyn wants it to be perfect. How can she run a gallery if she can't even organise a suburban birthday party?

Shoving the last bag of corn chips into the pantry she picks up her plate of crackers and cheese and takes it to the living room. She is completely exhausted because Harper was in her room at 5 a.m., needing to share a very ''portant' dream with her in which she had learned how to fly.

What will happen when Harper no longer wants to share her dreams? For so many years she has either been a mother or pursuing motherhood. Why does this have to be so hard? It doesn't seem that hard for other women.

Finishing the last bite of her cracker she contemplates getting up and getting some chocolate, but then she swings her legs around and lies down on the sofa. She'll think about all this once the party is over. Just before her eyes close, she texts Leah and asks if she's coming over in the morning to help decorate. Maybe a day spent with her old friend is just what she needs. They can prepare for the party and share a couple of drinks and laugh about being 'old'. She is asleep before she receives a reply from Leah.

———

Are you coming over tomorrow to help set up for the party?

Leah replies to the message from Katelyn with a thumbs up and a smiley emoji. Everything is all right here, her text seems to say. But it's not all right.

When she and Katelyn were sixteen, they both wrote a list of how they wanted their lives to be when they were thirty-six. They had written the lists on Leah's strawberry-scented pink notepaper, giggling as they covered their words from each other until they were ready to share.

By then, Leah had not been able to imagine a time in her life without Katelyn. Some weeks she slept over for three or four nights in a row and her parents basically treated her like a daughter. She even had to help load the dishwasher and set the table, like Leah did.

They had chosen the age of thirty-six because it seemed impossibly far into the future and also a very sophisticated age for a woman. Twenty-six still seemed quite young. Leah had a twenty-six-year-old cousin and she was only just beginning her career. She was a doctor but she still seemed very young. Both girls had agreed that by thirty-six a woman should have her life completely together and also have everything she wanted and dreamed of.

'Are you ready to show me?' Katelyn asked excitedly as she finished making her list.

'Wait,' said Leah. 'Let's read it out to each other one at a time and see how many we have exactly the same answer for.'

'Okay, me first,' shouted Katelyn gleefully.

Leah let her friend go first because she always let Katelyn do what she wanted to do.

'Right, what's first?' she asked.

'Let's do career. I'm going to have a fabulous career running a small gallery where the rich and famous come to buy paintings and sculptures.'

'Ooh, I bet you will. I am going to have a job that pays me enough so that I can dress in amazing clothes. Maybe something in fashion or like with a make-up company.'

'I knew you would put that,' laughed Katelyn. 'Now marriage, yes or no and who?'

'You go first.'

'Fine, I will be married to a man with brown hair and brown eyes because that's what I love and he will be something like a doctor or a lawyer or an accountant.'

'That is unbelievably boring. I will be married to an actor with black hair and green eyes. He will be incredibly famous but only love me,' said Leah, fluttering her eyelids and laughing.

'Do you want kids? I want at least four.'

'Hmm, maybe, definitely one. I mean he will be beautiful and I'm pretty so we have to have at least one child.'

'You are so vain, Leah Randall,' giggled Katelyn. 'I'm going to live in a mansion in the suburbs and have two dogs and I will bake every Saturday.'

'God, you are sooo boring. I'm going to live in the city and go to nightclubs every night and try every expensive restaurant I can find.'

'But will you still talk to me?'

'Of course I will, you're my best friend.'

Leah's house was set three blocks back from the ocean and afterwards they had taken their lists and gone on a favourite walk to a cliff at the end of a street that was a sheer drop of jagged grey-green rocks into the foaming ocean. Together they had stood solemnly side by side and ripped the lists into pieces, flinging them into the ocean and watching as the summer breeze caught bits of pink notepaper to carry off into the world.

'Promise me that no matter what happens we'll be friends forever,' said Katelyn and Leah had taken her hand and squeezed. 'Best friends forever,' she said and then they had giggled and run home again to make chocolate chip cookies.

They're still friends. That's the one thing that was on both of their lists, that they would both be friends forever.

But it feels like Katelyn has ticked off just about everything on her list, whereas Leah is sitting in her apartment, wondering how to tell people she's been fired as she pages through a wedding album, looking at pictures of a man she is no longer married to.

She has no idea how she got here and no idea what to do now. And tomorrow she will have to spend the day helping Katelyn decorate and watching Katelyn with her perfect husband and perfect child complain about all that perfection and how hard it is.

'Stop being such a bitch,' she mutters to herself, before she drops the album on the coffee table and stands to get herself another cup of coffee.

She adds a lot of milk and a dash of whisky to the coffee because she has literally nowhere to go at all and drinks it down quickly because it's lukewarm. And then she lies down on her sofa to have a nap because that's what you do when your life has fallen apart so spectacularly. You drink alcohol in the afternoon and you take a nap.

At least if she goes over to help decorate she will get to spend some time with Toby and Harper. Something she would never share with anyone is the fantasy she has sometimes about Katelyn simply disappearing. She can imagine stepping into the role of wife to Toby and mother to Harper so perfectly.

'How could that happen,' she mumbles aloud as the whisky loosens her muscles and her eyes close.

She dreams of lying next to Toby, his arms around her and a smile on his lips. Katelyn doesn't appear in the dream because, in the dream, Katelyn no longer exists.

TWENTY-FIVE

KATELYN

She gasps, struggling up from the darkness and taking a deep shuddering breath, her vision fuzzy as she opens her eyes and looks around. Where is she? Where the hell is she? She starts to move before she knows what to do, panic running through her. What's happened? Her memory is gone again, again.

'You're okay, you're okay,' she hears Toby say and feels his hand on her shoulder as he comes to stand next to her. 'Don't move and don't panic. You're in a hospital bed, just relax and take a deep breath. I'm right here, I promise you. Everything is okay.'

Katelyn lies back down, feeling the familiar starched sheets and hearing the crinkle of plastic, as she inhales deeply and then lets out her breath. She closes her eyes and repeats the action, hoping that at some point, she will get some clarity. The last thing she remembers is... she can feel her heart beginning to race as she struggles to recall what happened. She cannot be here again. It wasn't supposed to happen again. Trying for another deep breath she coughs and then puts her hands up to her throat where it burns and everything comes rushing back at her in a series of terrible images. Aaron with his teeth bared, his face red, his hands around her neck. 'Oh God,' she says, opening her eyes and sitting up.

Toby squeezes her shoulder. 'You kind of passed out again,' he says, fear and worry on his face. 'They're going to run some tests. Do you know where you are? How you got here? Can you tell me what you remember?'

'Toby,' she hears Maureen's voice, 'stop firing questions at her, stop it.' Katelyn turns her head to see her mother-in-law sitting in a chair. 'I came to check on you and that terrible man was...' She brushes her hand across her cheek, wiping away tears. 'Oh, it was just awful.'

'But you stopped him, Mum,' says Toby.

'How?' asks Katelyn, her voice burning her throat. 'How did you stop him? I thought he was going to kill me.'

'You do remember, you do,' says Toby, his voice light with relief.

'Yes,' says Katelyn. 'He came over... he wanted to talk and then when I asked him to leave, he got so angry and then he... I thought I was dying. How did you stop him?'

'When you didn't answer the door, I was so worried I used my key and there you were, your legs were moving but he was over you and his hands... and I got such a fright. I had left Ted in the car because I thought I would only be a moment. I screamed and then he turned and I... I was so scared I picked up the closest thing to me and it was that vase, the blue and green one I bought you for your first anniversary, and... and I hit him with it.' She moves her hands, demonstrating the action.

As her mother-in-law speaks, she flushes, her brown eyes shining with wonder at her own bravery. 'I know you liked that vase,' she says and Toby laughs.

'You saved her, Mum. You're a hero. Don't worry about the vase.'

'Yes,' agrees Katelyn. 'But I don't understand why he was so... Leah was married to him and... I just don't understand. He was your friend, Toby, your friend.'

Toby looks at his mother. 'Mum, can you give us a minute?' he says and Maureen nods.

'I'll go and call an Uber.'

'Harper,' says Katelyn, terror in her heart.

'She's still fast asleep, love. Ted's with her and I'll go there now. We'll stay until Toby comes home. Don't worry, we're here for you.' In the glaring light of the hospital room her mother-in-law looks older and exhausted and Katelyn is stabbed with guilt at what she has done to the people who love her, at how much she has put them through.

'Thank you, thank you,' she rasps, reaching out for Maureen's hand and squeezing hard.

'Of course, darling, of course,' she says, swiping at her face again and then she leaves.

Toby pulls up a chair and sits down next to her. 'I know what happened at the party, Katelyn. I've known all along. Leah told me when she caught you. She came and told me and I was so devastated... I don't know why you would... I mean, I thought you were happy... we were happy. It was so... I felt like I'd lost you and lost Aaron because he obviously wasn't a mate at all... I don't know how he could have and then your memory... Why did you do it, Kate? Why?'

Toby is pale in the harsh light of the hospital room, his eyes bloodshot with weariness.

Katelyn cannot explain, cannot excuse what she did, even though she doesn't remember it. 'I'm so sorry, Toby,' she says, feeling the sting of Leah's betrayal, but understanding it as well. She would probably have done the same thing if she caught Leah and Toby together. Anger would have driven her straight to Aaron if the two of them were still married. It's a huge betrayal of both her marriage and her friendship and she cannot explain it away. She nearly lost her life because of it. But she wants to find a way forward with her husband, she has to for Harper's sake and because she loves him. But she also needs to know the truth about him and Leah.

'I have an image in my mind, Toby, an image of you hugging Leah, not like a friendship hug but something else and maybe I made it up or... but it's there.'

Katelyn waits as the silence in the room grows larger. 'I did hug, Leah,' he says. 'The night of your party, after she told me what happened. I hugged her but I don't understand how you remember that if you can't remember anything else.'

'Sometimes, some stuff comes back. The neurologist said that flashes of memory were possible.' She coughs and he picks up a glass of ice water and hands it to her, watching her as she sips through a straw, feeling the wonderful relief of the cold water.

'What's going to happen now, Kate?' he asks and for a moment he seems very young and very unsure. She feels the same way. But the one thing she is sure of is that she can't lose him.

'I have no idea what happened at the party. I know what Aaron said and what Leah told you but also... I'm not sure I wanted anything to happen.'

'What do you mean?'

'Last night Aaron said that I was being a tease, that I was saying "no" when I meant "yes"' – she waves her hand – 'something like that. I'm just not sure that I was as willing... as willing to have sex with him as he says I was.'

'Bastard,' mutters Toby. 'Bastard, bastard, bastard.'

'But I don't know... I will probably never know.'

'We need to talk to the police,' says Toby firmly.

'No.' Katelyn shakes her head. 'No... he's been arrested for his attack on me, hasn't he?'

'Yes, yes. Mum called the police but he needs to be... I

didn't know what kind of a man he was. I would never have exposed you to him, had him in our house if I had known.'

'I know, I know.' Katelyn takes Toby's hand, squeezes. 'I don't want to talk about what happened at the party. I'll never be able to say for sure that I didn't want to do what I did. I've been feeling so... trapped,' she says, 'and he was offering me a way out, something for myself. I was going to tell you, I was—'

'What are you talking about?' asks Toby.

'Aaron and I have been meeting...' she begins and then because she can feel him rising out of his chair, his body tight with anger, she holds up her hand. 'Let me finish. We have been meeting to discuss him funding me opening a gallery. That is all I have done. What happened at the party was a one-time thing, I know that for sure. I was going to tell you about it, about the gallery, the day after the party but...' She cocks her head to the side and looks at him, knowing she doesn't have to explain why she didn't tell him.

Toby leans forward in his chair and drops his head into his hands.

'Are you telling me the truth?' he asks, his voice muffled by his hands.

'I am,' says Katelyn simply. 'I wanted to be more than just a mother and he was going to help me do that. But it was all a lie. He was never going to help me. I'm so sorry. Please say you'll forgive me for keeping that from you and for the party, for everything. I'll do anything, anything to make it right.' She coughs again, her throat is on fire. She moves to pick up her water again and Toby stands, holding the cup so she can drink.

'It's going to hurt to talk and swallow for a bit.'

'It feels like my throat is actually on fire,' she whispers, sipping some more water.

'He's always had a thing for you,' he says. 'Always... but I never thought... The police are going to want to interview you

when you're able. You need to tell the police what he did was...'
Katelyn can hear that Toby doesn't want to say the word.

'I know what happened when he came over, but I will never
be sure what happened at the party. Can you imagine how hard
it will be for me to prove anything? He'll use my TGA against
me. There was no one there but me and him and Leah... Leah
saw us and she thought—' Katelyn stops speaking. Toby is a
lawyer. She doesn't need to explain this to him.

'Then we leave it, you leave it, I mean. But he attacked you
last night. My mother saw it and it should be enough to get him
put away for a while.'

Katelyn nods. 'Did Leah know?' she asks, unable to comprehend that it may be possible. 'Did Leah know what he was
going to do?'

Toby shakes his head. 'No, no, of course not. I don't know
how he knew you were alone.'

'He said Leah told him,' Katelyn says, Aaron's words returning. 'He knew you were at Leah's apartment.'

Toby walks away, takes some steps around the room,
swinging his arms and she can see anger brewing.

'I don't know what to think but I've told her to stay away. I
called her and told her what happened and I asked her to come
but then... I called again and told her to stay away. But she's
here anyway. This has all gotten so completely out of control
and I just want it to stop now. She's your best friend, Kate.
What happened at the party broke her heart but she still loves
you and I don't think she meant for you to get hurt, but I don't
know... maybe Aaron lied.' He stops walking and looks at her
and then he shrugs his shoulders. 'I don't know anything
anymore; I feel like I just don't know what to think. I believe
Leah's a good person going through some stuff. She's lost her job
and things have been really bad for her.'

Neither she nor Toby want to believe that Leah told Aaron
that Katelyn was alone but how else would he have known?

'Even if she told him I was in the house on my own, she could never have expected him to do what he did,' says Katelyn. She believes this to be true. She has known Leah her whole life. Leah would never put Katelyn's life in danger and she certainly would never do anything to hurt Harper.

'Maybe Leah and I are both in the middle of some midlife crisis,' says Katelyn ruefully and she raises her hand to her head where a sharp pain makes her wince.

'You need to sleep,' says Toby. 'Maybe what the doctor said was true, you were already in the middle of the TGA when the party began and then you had all that alcohol... who knows what that did to your brain. I think we just need to leave it now.'

'Aaron said that I told him I hadn't had anything to drink at all, isn't that strange? I mean, it was my party. Obviously, I would have had something to drink.'

Toby shrugs. 'I think that we need to figure out why it happened. I don't want to lose you but something is wrong with us... something... I feel like you're distant, not just in the last few days but for months. But it's all a conversation for another time. You need to rest and I need to go home and relieve Mum and Dad.'

Katelyn nods and slides down in the bed, positioning the pillow behind her neck.

There is a light knock at the door to the hospital room and a nurse comes in, the same nurse who had treated Katelyn only days before. Amanda.

'You must like me very much,' Amanda says lightly, giving Katelyn's hand a squeeze and peering at her neck. Katelyn lifts her hand to the skin there, feeling a bruise already forming.

'It's very sore,' she says.

'You're going to be fine,' says Amanda, 'and your levels are good as well. The on-call obstetrician will be by soon to give you a scan.'

'Obstetrician?' says Katelyn.

And at the same time, Toby says, 'A scan for what?'

'Oh,' says Katelyn, remembering the pregnancy test she took but never got to look at because Aaron arrived.

'You didn't know?' asks Amanda and Katelyn shakes her head, feeling her eyes fill with tears. 'I didn't... I mean we had IVF for Harper and...'

Amanda pats her hand and smiles. 'Well I've heard of that happening. HCG levels are very good for around five or six weeks pregnant and the scan will tell us more.'

'Thank you,' says Katelyn because she wants Amanda to leave. Toby is silent, sitting in a chair, wringing his hands. He knows she doesn't want another child. She was adamant. But now they are here. Did she know she was pregnant at the party? Is that where the other pregnancy test went? It was possible and, if so, would it explain the TGA? The enormous stress she felt over having to go through it all again might have just pushed her over the edge. The more she thinks about it, the more possible it seems.

Amanda, sensing the tension in the room, leaves and they are alone.

Katelyn lets a thousand words circle in her head, unsure which ones to choose.

'What... what are you going to do?' Toby asks finally and Katelyn turns to look at her husband. He is putting the decision in her hands, knowing that she may make a choice that devastates him.

On the wall, a clock tells Katelyn that it's after 1 a.m. and she would like to sleep, to leave this night behind her, but she has no idea what she will wake up to. Her hand goes to her belly where a baby is growing. Still growing even after everything that has happened. Can she do this again? Can she do it again and will Toby be there for her the way she needs?

'I'm... going to be a mother to two children,' she whispers.

Toby sits up and crosses his arms across his chest, protecting his heart. 'Okay,' he says, wary.

'Okay?'

'Okay, we have to see someone, talk about this more but we're a family, you and me and Harper and whoever this is,' he says, gesturing at her hands on her belly, 'and that's how we're going to stay.'

Katelyn bursts into noisy tears of relief. She never had a real family before Toby. She borrowed Leah's all the time but it was never her family. Losing Toby would be like losing her mother all over again and she lost her mother so many times in her life, until she finally lost her forever.

'I'll be better this time,' she says through sobs as he stands and puts his arms around her. The decision has been made without her letting herself think about it. This baby is an apology of sorts to Toby. He wants a child and she wants him and she just hopes that she can do it better this time.

'We'll be better,' says Toby as though hearing her thoughts. 'We both will.'

TWENTY-SIX

LEAH

Wednesday, 1 a.m. – Four Days After the Party

It is one in the morning. In her car she tilts her head back against the seat and closes her eyes. How has it come to this?

She is in the hospital parking lot, again. Inside, Katelyn is lying in a hospital bed, again. But this time she has not driven with her friend to get her help and this time she has been told by Toby, 'Stay away.' He knows she's here anyway and here she will stay, until he lets her see Katelyn.

Toby sent Maureen to check on Katelyn when Katelyn wasn't answering her phone. Maureen has a key and so when she rang the bell and Katelyn didn't answer, she immediately used her key. And now Katelyn is lying in a hospital bed and Toby is with her and Leah is sitting alone in her car. And Aaron has been arrested. How has it come to this?

It was supposed to be an easy set-up. Leah lures Toby to her flat, giving Aaron a chance to talk to Katelyn, and then Toby comes home and finds the two of them together, hopefully in a compromising position.

But instead, Katelyn had only wanted Aaron gone and Aaron had attacked her, actually attacked her.

Something you don't know, Aaron told her over text when she asked him to get involved in her plan, *is that she and I have been seeing each other for a few months.*

Leah read those words and heard ringing in her ears. Katelyn and Aaron had been having an affair for months?

It wasn't enough that Katelyn still allowed Aaron to come to her house – despite how badly Leah's marriage had ended – she had to sleep with him as well? She hadn't asked him for any more details, she didn't care, didn't want to know. But she had felt justified in her plan. Toby belonged with someone who valued him.

While she waited for Toby to arrive, applying make-up and making sure her hair looked perfect, Leah had been unable to get the image of Katelyn and Aaron together out of her mind, seeing them not just at the party but in his bed too, in the bed that had been theirs once, together. And then she had suddenly felt sick. Katelyn was pregnant and it was probably Aaron's child because Katelyn was the kind of woman men had children with. Leah had wanted to curl up in her bed but a shot of vodka had kept her resolved. Toby would want to have a child with her, she was sure of it.

Her anger at Aaron for sleeping with her best friend sat in the back of her mind, just simmering. There was nothing she could do anyway. They were divorced.

But if what Aaron said was true, if he and Katelyn had been seeing each other for some time, why did he attack her?

Leah picks up her phone and texts Toby. *How is she? Please let me come up and see her.*

Stay out of our lives Leah. Just stay away.

'Not likely,' Leah mutters as she starts her car for the drive home. She has known Katelyn for longer than Toby has. She may have lost a husband and a job and a potential lover, but there's no way she's going to lose her best friend as well. She'll find a way back into Katelyn's life, back into Harper's life and Toby's life. She'll find a way.

TWENTY-SEVEN

KATELYN – THE NIGHT OF THE PARTY

Katelyn sits on the edge of the bathtub staring down at the pregnancy test. How can this be? How can this possibly have happened? She's on the pill. She's careful, so how did this happen? The word 'pregnant' glares out in bright blue.

This cannot be, it cannot happen. She just can't do this.

Downstairs the house is ready for her thirty-sixth birthday party. She hasn't had a drink yet because she was waiting until she had finished getting dressed but also because... she suspected this. Over the last few weeks, she has begun recognising the feelings that she had when she was pregnant with Harper. Her slight queasiness, the smell of coffee not attracting her like it always does and wine tasting weird. She has noticed but not noticed because it is her worst-case scenario.

Harper is at preschool three days a week now and next year it will be full-time and then she will be at school and it will be five days a week and Katelyn will be free again. Free to open a gallery with Aaron's help, to have lunch with interesting artists, to use her degree the way she had always dreamed of doing, to be Katelyn the person and not just Katelyn the wife, or Katelyn the woman who is desperately trying to get pregnant, or Katelyn the unhappy mother.

'Happy birthday, Katelyn,' she mutters as she looks down at the test.

She is weary with the knowledge of what will happen now. Toby won't let her terminate a pregnancy but will he hate her if the depression is the same as last time? What if she becomes that weird woman again who can't sleep or eat? What will happen to Harper if she checks out again?

Today she is thirty-six but her life is nothing like the way she imagined it. She remembers writing up a list with Leah on where they wanted to be at this age. She has the lawyer husband but only one child and no dog and no career. Her happiness is like the list she wrote, only paper thin. She hasn't slept for the last few nights as she goes over all the things that need to be done for the party, which is ridiculous. It's just a party for a woman on her way to middle age with nothing to show for her life except one child.

You are such a waste of space. Something her mother used to say to her in the middle of the benders when she got in the way or asked for dinner. Her mother was right. She is a waste of space who is terrible at being a mother, at being a wife, at being a person. Her head pounds and she would like to curl up under her duvet for the rest of the night.

She finds some tablets in the drawer of the bathroom cabinet and swallows them with water from the tap, cupping her hand under the stream. She would love a drink right now, many, many drinks, in fact, but she can't do that. Once again, her life is controlled by something else. Resentment floods her body and she touches her stomach, wishing it were not the truth. The diamond from her engagement ring flashes in the light and, irritated, she pulls off all her rings, going into the bedroom to place them next to her bed. Back in the bathroom she looks down at the test again and then at her hands. Once, she had been single. Free. She'll never be free again.

But she has a party to attend and so she puts the test into the bottom drawer of the bathroom cabinet. The guests will be arriving soon. She'll look at it later, think about it later. The only thing she needs to do is not drink, but that's not a problem since alcohol turns her stomach these days anyway.

Checking her make-up in the mirror she hears her mother's voice, 'You're going to end up alone like I was.'

Somewhere close she can feel a future where she is lying on a sofa and Harper is trying to take care of herself. It doesn't make sense because that would never happen but she can feel it there and suddenly... nothing makes sense at all.

Looking at herself in the mirror she blinks, thinking, 'What was I doing?' and then she hears some noise downstairs and goes to see what it is.

TWENTY-EIGHT

Saturday Night, 27 May, 11.15 p.m.

Leah stands with her arms folded, not bothering to start cleaning up, the bright lights of the living room making her wince.

In the hallway, yet another guest says, 'Goodbye, that was amazing, sure we can't stay to help you clean up?'

'No, all good thanks,' says Toby and then the front door shuts and it is just the three of them. Katelyn is sitting on the sofa, absent-mindedly scrunching the white tablecloth and releasing it, smoothing it out. It's unusual that she is not already in full cleaning mode but then nothing about this night is usual.

Toby comes into the room. 'God, what a mess,' he says, looking around.

'In more ways than one,' says Leah.

Katelyn stands and offers her a small smile. 'Hey, Leah,' she says. 'You look nice.'

'Are you joking?' asks Leah. 'After everything you did tonight, you have nothing but "hey, Leah, you look nice," to offer?'

'What did I do?' Katelyn looks genuinely confused.

'You... you screwed my ex-husband,' spits Leah, the ugly words spilling out of her mouth.

'Listen, Leah,' says Toby, holding up his hands. 'Maybe now is not the time... I think Kate and I need to be alone...'

'What are you talking about?' asks Katelyn, looking around the room at the chaos.

'I saw you,' yells Leah. 'I saw the two of you in the bathroom. You know I did.'

'I don't understand,' says Katelyn.

'You and Aaron,' says Toby. 'She saw you.'

'Saw me what? What are you talking about?'

'God, how drunk are you, Katelyn? Who screws someone else and doesn't remember?' says Toby through gritted teeth, looking past his wife to the banner that has lost its grip on the wall. Leah can see that he cannot look at his wife. Good. He shouldn't look at her.

Katelyn looks around the room. 'What's happened here?' she asks. 'Why is it such a mess? What time is it? Where's Harper?'

'How drunk are you?' Toby replies, shaking his head.

'I'm not drunk,' she says. 'Why would I be drunk? Why on earth is everything such a mess? I'm having my party here in...' She looks around. 'Where's my phone? What's the time? The guests are coming at seven. How can they be here with such a mess?'

'Really funny, Katelyn, that's really funny,' hisses Toby.

Leah stands away from them, letting them have their argument. She has a lot to say, a lot, but she will wait. Let them tear each other apart. She puts a hand to her chest where there is pain over her heart. Normally she would be cleaning up, helping get the room back to how it was the day before, but she doesn't want to touch anything. The mess feels right because everything should be chaos. Everything is chaos.

Katelyn repeats her question and Toby and Leah share a look.

'Do you think this is some kind of alcoholic blackout?' she asks Toby as though Katelyn isn't standing right there.

Toby shrugs his shoulders and folds his arms, the sides of his mouth dropping, making him look older than he is.

'Stop messing around, Katelyn,' says Leah firmly.

'I'm not messing around. Why is it such a mess in here? My party starts at seven.'

'It's the alcohol definitely,' says Leah. 'She's obviously had a fortune to drink.'

'I haven't had a drink. Why is this place such a mess, the guests will be here in... Where's my phone? What's the time?'

'Katelyn, the party is over,' snaps Toby. 'Everyone has gone home.'

'What, why's this place such a mess? The guests will be here soon. What's the time? Where's my phone?'

'Stop screwing around, Katelyn,' shouts Toby, his face reddening.

'Why are you shouting at me?' Katelyn asks tearfully. 'Why's the house such a mess?'

'Really, you're worried about the mess?' Toby is standing by the trestle table where all the drinks were lined up at the beginning of the evening and he swings his hand, connects with a half-empty champagne bottle, tipping it onto its side, pale yellow liquid seeping out onto the blue rug underneath, a dark stain spreading. 'There's more mess now.'

'Look what you've done, look at this mess,' she screams. She turns around and then back again.

'Me?' he answers. 'Me?' Fury in his voice. 'What about what you've done? What about what you did?'

'I don't know what you're talking about. What are you talking about?'

'How drunk are you?' he spits.

'Look at this mess,' she repeats.

'Are you crazy?' he asks. 'Are you crazy or just trying to drive me crazy?'

'What do you mean? Look at this mess.'

'Stop yelling at me. This is your fault.'

'What are you talking about?' Katelyn asks again.

Toby steps forward, grabs his wife by the shoulders and shakes her a little. 'How much have you had to drink tonight?' he growls.

Katelyn shakes him off. 'Stop that, Toby. Why are you saying this?' She steps back and steps on a plastic cup, the cracking sound of plastic shattering loud in the empty silent house.

Katelyn blinks.

'What's happening here?'

'I can't deal with this,' says Toby. Shaking his head. 'You need to sleep it off, Katelyn.'

'Sleep what off? Why is this such a mess? I'm having my party here. The guests are arriving any minute.'

'Katelyn, are you insane?' asks Toby.

'What are you talking about? Why is this house such a mess? The guests are arriving any minute.'

Leah steps forward and pushes her face close to Katelyn's, looking for subterfuge, for some evidence that she is lying or that she is even, horrifyingly, joking, but Katelyn's green eyes are filled with confusion.

'Katelyn, are you okay?' she asks.

'Why are you asking me that?' She looks around the room. 'Why is this place such a mess? The guests will be arriving any minute.'

Leah looks at Toby again and watches his face change, a flicker of worry crossing his features as he uncrosses his arms.

He steps forward again and puts his hands on Katelyn's shoulders, forcing her to look at him. 'Katelyn, how much have you had to drink tonight?' he enunciates slowly, as though Katelyn is having trouble hearing him.

Round and around they go for ten minutes, the conversation circling back on itself until Toby says, 'I think something is wrong with her. I don't think this is alcohol. It may be... I don't know, a stroke or something. We need to take her to the hospital.'

In an instant he has switched into protective husband mode, fear making him pale. But Leah can see that there is also a touch of relief there. A stroke would be terrible but it would explain some things, things that threatened the lives of all three of them.

Leah is sobering up quickly. But Toby doesn't care about her. All that matters is what is wrong with Katelyn.

'Katelyn, smile,' she says and Katelyn obliges, bewildered. 'Now lift your arm, right arm and left arm. Walk over here,' she barks, fear making her harsh. How can Katelyn have a stroke? Old people have strokes, not thirty-six-year-old women.

'Why are you asking me to do this? Where's my phone? What's the time... the guests will be here soon.'

'Right, we're going to the hospital,' says Toby. 'The car is unlocked in the garage. Get her in there while I grab my wallet.'

Leah wants to suggest an ambulance but it feels safer to get to the hospital as soon as they can.

'Get her into the car,' yells Toby as he searches for his keys.

'Where are we going?' asks Katelyn as Leah pushes her towards the garage, physically making her move.

'We need to see a doctor.'

'Why?'

'Because of you, Katelyn,' Leah says, opening the car door as she shivers in the cold air of the garage and pushing her friend into the car.

They speed through silent streets, Toby driving, Leah and Katelyn in the back seat.

The windows fog up as the heater warms the car against the

cold autumn air. Outside, a strong wind pushes brown leaves along pavements, making Leah shiver at the thought of how cold it will be once they are out of the car. They hadn't thought to grab their coats.

Leah squeezes Katelyn's hand, watching her friend wipe tears from her face, streaking her thick mascara. There is such despair in her green eyes, such confusion.

'Where are we going?' Katelyn asks.

'To the hospital,' says Leah.

Katelyn runs her hand through her hair, pulling and tangling. 'Why?'

'Because something is wrong with you,' sighs Leah. She focuses on Toby who is driving, his eyes on the road and his body slightly hunched over the steering wheel. Looking at her friend, she can see, even just by looking at the back of his head, that he has somehow found a way to push everything else that has happened out of his mind in order to just get to the hospital safely. His emotions swirl around him but his gaze remains fixed on the road, his jaw tense, his shoulders hunched near his neck.

'Where are we going?' Katelyn asks.

'To the hospital,' repeats Leah. She squeezes Katelyn's hand again.

'We'll be there in ten minutes,' says Toby, the words clipped, anger fermenting underneath the simple expression of time.

'Am I dying?' asks Katelyn.

Leah swipes at her own eyes, looks at her friend. 'No,' she says emphatically. 'You're not dying.'

'Where are we going?' asks Katelyn.

Leah bites down on her lip. 'We're going to the hospital because something is wrong with you,' she says.

'Nothing is wrong with me, don't be ridiculous. I'm fine.'

'You're not fine, Katelyn, something is wrong.'

'I want to go home, I'm tired.'

'You have to see a doctor first.'

'Where are we going?' In the dark, streetlights blend together with the movement of the car and Leah wonders if this is some surreal dream or if she is actually going crazy.

She sniffs, smells the wine she spilled on her top, tastes the remains of the spicy salsa she had kept eating with corn chips. She wants a shower and to brush her teeth. She wants to wash away the whole evening forever. She wants the party never to have happened.

'Where are we going?' asks Katelyn as Toby pulls into the parking lot in front of Emergency, large red letters letting them know they are in the right place.

'We're here,' he says, without turning around.

'Why are we here?' asks Katelyn.

'Because of you,' replies Leah, letting go of her friend's hand. 'All because of you.'

TWENTY-NINE

KATELYN

Three Months After the Party

As they walk, Katelyn can feel the folded shape of the letter in her pocket every time she brushes her fingers across her jeans.

She should have just thrown it out.

The late August air is icy and spring still feels very far away.

'Come on, slowpoke,' calls Leah. 'We have to get to the top before the storm comes.' Katelyn looks up at the gathering grey, the clouds moving in the wind, banking up together to cover every inch of sky.

'Maybe we should turn back,' she shouts above the wind. 'It looks like the rain will be here any minute.'

She has left Harper at Leah's parents' house, sitting on the sofa with Teresa watching *The Little Mermaid*. Teresa had been delighted to sit with the little girl while Katelyn and Leah went up to the cliff to talk. Leah has moved back in with her parents while she saves for a deposit to buy herself an apartment. She's in a new job but has had to take a pay cut and Katelyn knows that she is mortified by the fact that her boss is ten years younger than she is.

'I won't be there for long,' Leah has said. 'Just long enough to find my feet again.' Coming over to visit Leah at her parents' house makes Katelyn feel like a child again, but this time she has her own child in tow.

Why don't you come to me? Katelyn suggested over text.

Please just come over and then we can walk to the cliff. We can talk and it will feel like a new start.

There is no new start for her and Leah, but somehow Katelyn had not been able to refuse and so she is here and Teresa is happily minding Harper.

'Good for you girls to figure this all out,' she said, but right now Katelyn is regretting allowing Leah to talk her into coming over and she is also regretting letting Harper come with her. Toby is at work and today is not Harper's preschool day. She should have left this conversation for another time. There is a part of her that wants to get back the friendship she and Leah had, that wants to make everything the same again, even though, logically, she knows that can never happen.

But Leah has tried so hard, has persisted with apology texts and apology emails and checking in nearly every day, waiting for Katelyn to be ready to talk.

'I wish she would just stop,' Katelyn said to Toby last night when Leah suggested this.

'Maybe give her this last chance to say sorry, speak to her and tell her that we have to move on as a family. It will be easier and more final if you say it in person.'

'What if I still want to be friends?' Katelyn asked Toby. They were lying in bed with the lights out, both exhausted from the day and speaking quietly in case Harper was sleeping lightly.

'Then that's okay too,' said Toby. 'You do what feels right.'

Katelyn is not sure what feels right, not after everything, but she wants to hear what Leah has to say, even if it is for one final time.

Leah stops walking and looks up. 'We need to get to the top, Katelyn. We need to...' She doesn't finish her statement because she doesn't have to. The top of the cliff was where they pledged to be friends forever at sixteen and that's where they need to go again, to start again – if they even can.

Katelyn feels for the letter. Perhaps she can rip it up and throw it over the cliff like they did with their lists at sixteen.

'Hell hath no fury like a woman scorned,' was the way the saying went, but a man scorned was worse. Aaron's ego couldn't take her rejection of him and that's why he's now on bail, waiting for his trial, that's why Toby and Katelyn have taken out an apprehended violence order against him. He cannot come anywhere near them and he cannot contact them. Leah has vowed to never speak to him again. 'I can't believe it of him,' she has said many times in her messages over the last few months. Katelyn knows you can be married to someone and not know them at all. Marriages can be filled with secrets and lies, twisted and complicated. It's the same with friendships. She and Leah thought they knew each other, truly knew each other, but perhaps they don't. Perhaps you can never really know the truth about someone.

She should have taken the letter to the police and shown them but she has kept it instead.

She pushes against the wind to get to the top of the cliff, grateful for her black puffer jacket and the beanie she is wearing. There's a fence at the top now to stop people from going too close to the edge. It wasn't there when she and Leah were sixteen and they had loved sitting on the edge, dangling their legs over the cliff and staring down into the churning ocean. They were fearless at sixteen but now they know how easy it is to lose in life, to lose jobs and people and themselves. They are no longer fearless.

Walking faster, Katelyn briefly rests her hand on her stomach where she's already started to feel some movement. Harper has decided the baby is a boy, something they will be able to confirm next week at the eighteen-week ultrasound. Katelyn is excited for it, remembering her first glimpse of Harper, but at the same time she is terrified. What if something is wrong? What if everything is fine and after she gives birth, it's like the last time? What if she's not up to the task of mothering two children?

'It won't be like last time,' Toby keeps telling her and he has already tentatively booked in a night nurse for two weeks after the birth. It's expensive but so is therapy and drugs and now Katelyn is a mother already and she cannot stop mothering Harper. She still has moments of fantasising about the gallery, wondering what it would have been like, but she keeps reminding herself that the gallery was a ruse, a way to get close to her. There was never going to be a gallery. And when the baby moves, tiny bubbles inside her, she feels a special joy for what is to come. After everything they went through to have Harper, this baby is a miracle in many ways. Katelyn is trying to view it as a miracle whenever her fear rears up and threatens to choke her.

Harper has become clingier since she found out about the baby. She is only three and still trying to make sense of her mother being in hospital, not once but twice. She and Toby are still using the 'sore head' excuse, as they try to figure out what would be the best thing to say.

'Should we speak to someone about it?' Toby asked last night over dinner when Harper was reluctant to go and watch television, something that she always loved. 'Maybe get a therapist to talk to her? I mean, she doesn't leave you alone for a second.'

'I think I'm going to give it some more time. She needs to be with me and that's okay. She's still going to school. She just needs to feels safe,' Katelyn replied.

'I guess that's what everyone wants,' Toby said and then he threw her a quick smile. Some days it feels as though she and Toby are exactly who they seem to be – a happy couple expecting their second child. Other days it feels as though that image is a thin veneer that will easily peel off, leaving her without her husband. But they are trying. They are both trying.

Today is about Leah, about the two of them trying to navigate a new way forward.

A walk to their favourite childhood spot feels right, like they are going back to a time before the party.

No matter how many times she goes back to the night of the party, she cannot remember what happened and she probably never will, but she's grateful for the lost hours now. Having the memory would have been tormenting and the TGA allowed her to take a step back, to take stock of her life and realise that she needed to be grateful for what she had. She is trying to remember that, even on the hard days.

Seeing that she was pregnant after the stress of planning for the party and her unhappiness in her life led to the TGA – she's sure of it. Suddenly it was just all too much and so her brain just checked out. Aaron took advantage of that without even knowing it was happening to her. He took advantage and she was not strong enough or present enough to fight him off, to scream, to run. But she cannot hold him accountable because she doesn't remember it. His attack on her will be enough to send him to jail for a long time, she hopes.

Leah is at the top of the cliff now, standing in front of the fence. 'Come on,' she calls and as she does, Katelyn hears a shout of 'Mummy, wait for me.'

She turns, shocked to see that Harper is running up the cliff as fast as her little legs can go. She is wearing her red coat but it's unzipped and her matching red beanie is clutched in her hand.

'Harper, what are you doing here?' she yells. 'How did you get here?'

Her daughter stops running and hangs her head as Katelyn makes her way back to her, crouching down when she gets close and she can see tears appearing. 'You left me behind,' says Harper with a sniff. 'I wanted to come on the walk and you left me.'

'But you were watching a movie with Teresa,' says Katelyn. 'She'll be worried about you.' As she speaks, she zips up Harper's coat and fixes the beanie on her head, moving the little girl's long chestnut hair away from her face.

'She wented to the bathroom and I ran away,' says Harper. 'You can't leave me, Mummy.'

'Oh, sweetheart,' says Katelyn, picking her daughter up. 'I'm not going to leave you, I promise. It was just a walk with Aunty Leah and it's cold. It's much nicer to be inside.' She turns to Leah. 'You'd better call your mum and tell her we have her. She'll be frantic.'

Leah nods and Katelyn watches her call her mother as she walks towards her. 'I think I should just go back now. Perhaps we can get coffee next week when she's at school.' Relief washes over Katelyn as she says this. It doesn't feel right to do this now, not when she knows that the conversation is going to be difficult.

There are things she wants to say that she doesn't want her daughter to hear.

'No,' says Leah. 'Please, let's just stay for a few minutes.'

Katelyn puts Harper down and the little girl runs to the chain-link fence and grasps the cold metal, staring out at the edge of the cliff. 'Look at the big waves.'

'It's so cold,' says Katelyn.

'But beautiful,' says Leah. Katelyn looks out at the ocean, a grey blue under the clouds that are heavy in the sky.

'Yes, it always has been,' she says.

'Remember that night that Jason broke up with me,' says Leah, as the wind whips around them and waves crash below.

Katelyn nods. 'I was so worried about you.'

'Who's Jason?' asks Harper, looking up at her mother.

'He was a mean boy who broke my heart,' says Leah, 'but your mum brought me up here and we ate a whole block of chocolate together and then I felt better.'

'I wish I had a chocolate,' says Harper, making both women laugh.

'I thought he was the love of my life,' Leah says ruefully.

'You were sixteen,' says Katelyn. 'Everything feels so intense at sixteen.'

'Should we sit on the edge?' says Leah.

'No way, there's a fence for a reason,' says Katelyn. 'And we're not going anywhere near that with this little one here.'

'I'm not little, I'm big,' says Harper petulantly.

'Of course you are,' says Leah and she climbs easily over the fence.

'Leah, what are you doing? That's crazy,' says Katelyn, her hands clammy as Leah peers over the edge of the cliff.

'Come on, Kate, for old time's sake. Sit on the edge with me.'

'No way,' says Katelyn, shaking her head.

'I'll go to the edge,' says Harper, jumping up and down, excited at the prospect of doing something that is obviously not allowed and before the words, 'Definitely not,' leave Katelyn's lips, Leah has leaned over and picked up Harper, taking her over the fence.

'What are you doing?' shrieks Katelyn. 'Give her back.'

'Come and get her, Kate.' Leah smiles and Katelyn feels a creeping fear at the way her friend is looking at her. Why would she do something so reckless? Without another thought, Katelyn clambers over the fence and stands next to Leah, reaching out her arms. 'Give her to me, please,' she says, trying not to let Harper see how scared she is.

Leah steps back, her arms wrapped tightly around Harper who giggles as though they are playing a game.

'Remember how freaked out my mum was every time we told her we were coming up here before they built the fence?' asks Leah, taking a tiny step back towards the edge of the cliff.

'I understand her now,' whispers Katelyn. 'Please, Leah, let me put her on the other side of the fence.'

'"You two will end up dead",' laughs Leah, her laugh high-pitched and slightly hysterical. 'Remember she used to say that?'

'She was worried about us, just like I'm worried about Harper being so close to the edge.' Katelyn speaks slowly, wanting to keep the situation calm. Leah is just trying to scare her. 'Your mum was so wonderful to me. She was always around to listen, even when she didn't like what we were saying. That's why she said we should talk. She's a great mother and I know she would say that we shouldn't be doing this. It's dangerous.'

'She loved you, still does,' says Leah, her eyes fixed on Katelyn's face. 'I know it's dangerous,' she says slowly and electric shocks of fear move through Katelyn's body. What is happening here?

'You're scaring me,' she says, keeping her tone even.

'But I'm just having fun. Aren't we having fun, Harper?' She jiggles the little girl in her arms.

'Fun,' says Harper, but she looks at the edge of the cliff and Katelyn can see that her child is sensing something. 'I want to go to Mum,' says Harper, reaching for her mother.

'Not yet,' says Leah, and she takes another step back. Katelyn can feel her heart in her throat. If she screams it will startle Leah and Harper, and if she lunges for her child and misses, Leah could step away and fall. The wind whips around them, cold and sharp, and time slows down as Katelyn watches her friend with her daughter.

'I'm so sorry, Leah,' says Katelyn carefully. 'I don't think I wanted what happened at the party. I don't but I can't remember any of it and all I know for sure is that I'm so sorry you got hurt.'

Leah looks straight at her. Katelyn has no idea what Leah is going to do now.

'I know you're sorry. I know you think you're sorry,' she says. Katelyn's mind whirls with things she could say to get Leah to climb back over the fence.

'Have you read the letter he sent you?' asks Leah, a touch of sadness in her voice.

'I want to go to Mum,' says Harper again.

'How did you...' begins Katelyn and Leah shrugs her shoulders.

'I saw it in your bag when you took Harper to the bathroom.'

'You went through my bag?'

'There was a time, Kate, when that wouldn't have bothered you at all.'

Katelyn lifts her arms, reaching for her child. 'It's fine, I don't mind. Did you read the letter?'

'No, you were only gone for a couple of minutes. Do you mind that I saw it, that I know about it?'

'Of course not...' The words stick in Katelyn's mouth. Once her child is back in her arms, she will never see Leah again. Looking around them, she prays for someone to come by and tell them to climb back over the fence, for something to distract Leah so she can grab her daughter.

'I have it with me... the letter, I brought it up here,' says Katelyn. 'I haven't read it and I don't think I want to read it, but I will if you want me to. We can read it together.' She will say anything to get a hold of her daughter, anything to have the child in her arms, safe from harm.

'Yes, I think we should read it together.' Leah nods, clutching Harper tighter as the little girl wriggles.

'Mum, Mum,' she says, reaching out and Katelyn opens her arms wider, but as she steps forward, Leah steps back again.

'Or I can just rip it up and throw it away the way we did with all the letters Jason wrote to you,' says Katelyn, dropping her arms, her stomach churning. 'We can gift it to the ocean.' She wants to rip it up, wants the words to disappear, wants everything that happened to have never been, but mostly she wants to feel her child in her arms.

'No, no,' says Leah. 'You should read it, read it aloud, and then we can tear it up and move on with our lives.' She smiles and Katelyn feels shivers run along her spine.

'Okay,' she says, leaning sideways slightly and pulling the envelope out of her pocket.

She unfolds the letter and takes the single page out of the envelope. The wind changes direction, making Katelyn think she will lose her grip on the piece of paper.

'You read it,' she says, extending her arm, the piece of paper flapping in the wind, and she watches as Leah hesitates, but she can see that her friend is desperate to know what the letter says.

'Okay,' says Leah, reaching for the paper and at the same time handing Harper to Katelyn. Katelyn steps back, squeezing her daughter tightly, her stomach filled with rising nausea and her breathing uneven. She moves right up to the fence and puts Harper down on the other side, peeling her daughter's arms off her body. 'Just let me climb back over, baby.'

'Not until we've read the letter,' commands Leah and Katelyn stops moving.

'Go and sit down on that stone, quickly,' says Katelyn curtly and Harper, sensing that something is wrong, runs a little way from the fence to where Katelyn has pointed. She needs to get back over the fence and then she will pick up her daughter and run. 'I better climb back over,' she explains to Leah but as she makes to climb over, Leah grabs her puffer jacket.

'No,' she says. 'We're going to read the letter. You stay right here,' and Katelyn can hear the threat in her words. Leah is probably stronger than she is and Katelyn is pregnant. A soft whimper escapes her lips, taken by the wind so Leah doesn't hear her terror. How can this be happening? What on earth is she going to do?

She looks at Leah, knowing that she needs to stay calm, that they both need to stay calm. 'Okay, I'll stay here while you read it.' She sticks her fingers through the links in the fence, holding on tightly to the icy metal.

'Read it, Leah,' she says, 'and then we can go back and this will all be over.'

THIRTY

LEAH

Three Months After the Party

Leah looks down at the paper flapping in her hand and for a moment she wants to run her fingers over the scrawled letters. Aaron always did have the worst handwriting. It was something they used to laugh about when they first started dating. It wasn't that long ago and yet it was an entirely different life and she was a completely different person to who she is today.

She has a feeling she knows what the words are going to be because even though they were only married for three years she knows her ex-husband hates to lose. His violence had always been simmering beneath the surface and it bubbled over the night he went to see Katelyn because he really, really hates to be told 'no'. Being told 'no' is the same as losing.

Leah hates to lose as well.

Aaron thought he knew her pretty well. He thought he knew whatever there was to know about her and Katelyn thinks the same thing, but both of them have underestimated her, both of them have underestimated how much she hates to lose and how determined she is not to lose, not to feel like a loser. And for the last couple of years, she has only felt like a loser. She wasn't going to hurt Harper, of course she wasn't, but she needed Katelyn to stay here, to be here in a place where they had declared they would be best friends forever.

Dear Katelyn, she begins, her eyes scanning the rest of the letter so she knows exactly what's coming. She knew anyway. She reads slowly, carefully, marvelling at how she manages to control her voice.

That's why they're here, her and Katelyn. Because she knew what Katelyn would do. She knew Katelyn would keep the letter for days and probably even end up throwing it out without looking at it, but Leah wants her to know what the words say. Katelyn can't run from the truth anymore. The TGA is over. Katelyn's memory is just fine now. It's best if the truth comes out.

> *I know you won't want to hear from me. I know I could never apologise enough for what happened but I just had to write once, only once.*
>
> *I loved you, Katelyn, I still do. I know that you will be blaming yourself for what happened because that's what you do but you have no idea, Katelyn, no idea about what the real truth is.*
>
> *Leah knew what I had planned. In fact, she encouraged me to give you the gift at the party, just like she encouraged me to start talking to you about the gallery months ago. She encouraged me to get you alone that Saturday night and we all know what happened then. You might say that Leah came up with the whole thing, but I have to admit my part in it. I've always had a thing for you, Katelyn, and I don't think Toby appreciates you enough. Leah's always known about how I felt. And I also know how she feels about Toby.*
>
> *'Wouldn't that be perfect,' she said to me when we got divorced. 'Katelyn and I could just swap lives and everyone*

*would be happier.' I think I laughed at the time, but whenever
we speak – and we speak more than you know – she brought it
up until I agreed. You have no idea what it was like to see you
every time I came over and not be able to touch you. We had a
plan, she and I. A stupid plan and I'm glad it didn't work but I
think I should warn you about her.*

Watch out for her, Katelyn – she doesn't mean you well.

Leah pushes her shoulders back as she reads Aaron's final
words. He could have just kept quiet but Leah had had a feeling
he would be throwing her under the bus as soon as he could.

Without waiting to hear what Katelyn has to say, Leah tears
the letter in half and in half again and again, until she is left
with nothing but small pieces, and she lifts her hands to the
wind and lets the air take her ex-husband's betrayal out to sea.
He's the one waiting for a trial. He's the loser, not her. She
won't be the loser again.

And then she turns to look at Katelyn whose green eyes are
wide with incomprehension, her mouth slightly open. Leah can
see she has no idea how to react.

Leah lets the silence between them grow as they gaze at
each other. The wind dies down and they are enveloped in the
stillness that exists between one wind gust and the next.

'We should go back,' says Katelyn slowly. 'I'm going to
climb back over now.' She turns away from Leah and lifts her
leg but Leah is not letting her get away with just pretending she
hasn't heard what Aaron said.

'No, we're staying,' says Leah firmly and she grabs at Katelyn's puffer coat, pulling her away from the fence and making
Katelyn stumble on some scattered stones.

'I know he's lying, Leah,' says Katelyn, righting herself,
standing straight and trying to pull away. 'Stop this,' she says
firmly. 'Obviously he's lying.'

Katelyn wants her to confirm that Aaron is indeed lying.

Katelyn wants to be able to put this behind them, to go back to her nice life with her lovely husband and daughter and a baby on the way and just pretend that she never tried to take what wasn't hers. Maybe she was in the middle of a brain snap, maybe she had no idea what she was doing, maybe she started something and then didn't want to finish it, but she still did it and that's not all Katelyn has taken from her.

'You know I used to hate it when you and my mother got together,' she says, her hands holding tightly on to the slippery material of Katelyn's puffer jacket.

'What do you mean?' asks Katelyn. She tries to take a step back towards the fence again but Leah steps forward, still holding on to the jacket, pulling her away. Katelyn looks over at Harper and looks back at her. Leah's not letting her get even a foot away from her.

'When you came over and she brought out her home-made cookies and then the two of you sat together discussing everything going on in your sad life – I hated that. It felt like you were taking her from me. She was always so interested in you, in everything you had to say, and she was never that interested in me.'

Katelyn laughs, sounding incredulous, moving her body to try and loosen Leah's grip on the jacket, but Leah holds on tighter. 'Rubbish, Leah,' she says. 'Your mother loves you more than anything. She was just nice to me because she felt sorry for me, that's all.'

Katelyn links her fingers in the fence again. Leah feels a rising fury inside her. How stupid does Katelyn think she is? They are at least six feet from the edge. She steps forward, right up to Katelyn, so close she can smell a faint scent of jasmine from the perfume Katelyn uses, even with the wind blustering around them.

'It felt like she liked you more but I was okay with that because I liked you so much, loved you really. It's been like that since we were six years old. I felt sorry for you at first, but then you were so sweet and so clever and everyone liked speaking to you but they mostly avoided me.'

'They were just jealous of you,' says Katelyn as Leah watches her hand tighten in the links of the fence. Katelyn glances over to where Harper is sitting again. The little girl is still, watching them both. Leah wishes she weren't here. She wasn't supposed to be here.

'You were my best friend. That's always been how I comforted myself whenever anyone paid more attention to you, or whenever you got something that I wanted. I loved you and I knew you loved me and we were best friends so I was happy because you were happy. Even when you got Toby, I was happy for you.'

'Leah,' says Katelyn and Leah can hear she's moving into her lecture voice, the one that she uses to keep Harper from misbehaving. 'Your mother adores you and you were always more popular than I was. And you broke up with Toby.'

'I know you know the truth about that,' says Leah. 'I know he would have told you.' She lets go of the jacket because her fingers are cramping and can see Katelyn visibly relax a little but her fingers remain tightly attached to the fence. 'He told you the truth, didn't he? He wouldn't have been able to help himself.'

Katelyn looks away, caught out in the lie.

'And you don't even love him the way you should. You've never been grateful for the things you have. You've always wanted more.'

The wind picks up again and Leah shivers a little. 'It seems to me that everything I ever wanted, you got. Even Aaron.'

Katelyn takes a deep breath. 'Leah, I've told you how sorry I am about that and I don't think I wanted that. In fact, I'm pretty sure I didn't.' She grabs the fence with her other hand, looking awkward as she contorts herself so she can look at Leah and hold on. 'I was going through something weird and I have no idea what happened. I lost my memory and I just... snapped. I don't remember any of it, but I do know that if I was in my right mind, none of that would have happened.'

'Maybe, but maybe it would have been for the best. Toby is wonderful and you don't appreciate him.'

'We should go back,' says Katelyn. 'I'm going to climb over now. We can talk back at your mum's house.'

'Everything Aaron said in the letter is true,' says Leah, the wind whipping her hair around her face.

Katelyn stops. 'What?' she asks, although she has obviously heard what Leah said.

'It's true and it's still true. You can forgive Aaron and drop the charges against him and you and Toby can... we can all still be friends. Maybe I can have a baby too.' Leah hates the terrible desperation she can hear in her voice but that's how she feels: desperate. She wants the fantasy she has been carrying for so long to become real. She has imagined the four of them sitting around a table together, laughing about how strange life is – Katelyn with Aaron, Leah with Toby, her hand resting on her belly where a child is growing.

'I...' begins Katelyn and then she shakes her head. 'I'm going home,' she says, turning around and lifting her leg to climb back over the fence, but Leah is not letting her go. She can feel Katelyn almost laughing at her for wanting what she has and it's not fair. None of this is fair.

'No,' she says, her voice rising as she grabs at Katelyn's coat and pulls her away from the fence. Katelyn is not as strong as she is. 'You're not just running away from this. My life is in ruins. I have nothing and I need you to help me. When you had nothing, I helped you.' She needs to make Katelyn understand.

'Let go, Leah,' says Katelyn, her tone strident with anger, her feet slipping over loose stones as she tries to pull away. 'You're being ridiculous.'

'Let my mummy go,' shouts Harper, jumping off the stone and running towards the fence, grabbing hold and starting to climb.

'No, baby,' yells Katelyn. 'Stay back, please, stay back. Let go, Leah, you don't want to do this.' She strains against Leah, pulling one way as Leah pulls her towards the edge.

'Stop it, Leah,' shouts Katelyn. 'You're crazy, this is crazy.'

And Leah does feel crazy, her mind a whirl of hideous emotions, her life in ruins, all her plans thwarted.

Leah stumbles on some gravel and turns to look behind her where the edge of the cliff is a jagged line of danger. Katelyn tries to pull back. 'Please, Leah,' she whimpers. 'Please don't do this.'

This wasn't the plan. The plan was to make Katelyn see that they could make a different arrangement work. Or was it? The last few months, the last few years come at Leah in images and she's unsure of exactly what she is doing or what she wants. The only thing she is clear about is that she does not want to feel this way anymore.

Leah loves Harper and Harper loves her, but Harper loves her mother more. Everyone loves Katelyn more.

'Let go, let go,' shouts Katelyn, and Leah can see she understands she is fighting for her life.

They are moving closer to the cliff edge; tiny amounts of sea spray, carried up by the wind as waves crash into the rocks below, hits their faces. A streak of lightning across the sky is followed by a rumble of thunder in the distance. The storm will be here soon.

Leah pulls Katelyn and Katelyn tries to pull away.

'Leah, please, please,' begs Katelyn as Leah moves her closer and closer to the edge.

'You're my best friend, Leah, I love you,' whispers Katelyn.

Leah searches her friend's face. Is that the truth? In Katelyn's green eyes she thinks she does see love and compassion and forgiveness, everything she wants, and as another rumble of thunder growls through the air, Leah stops pulling her oldest friend, relieved that everything feels clearer.

'I'm sor—' she begins to say.

'I know about you and Toby, you know,' says Katelyn, planting her feet wide, her teeth bared.

'Know what about me and Toby?' asks Leah, both her arms dropping to her sides. What has happened here? What is Katelyn talking about?

'I know you slept together when Harper was a baby.' Katelyn speaks quietly, almost too quietly for Leah to hear.

Leah sees herself on Saturday night, guiding Katelyn to the car so that they could take her to the hospital, her heart broken, her life devastated by everything that had happened. Toby had climbed into the driver's seat.

'I think I should sit in the back with her,' Leah said.

'Good idea,' he called.

'Where are we going?' asked Katelyn as Leah guided her into the car.

'The hospital,' said Leah, her heart heavy, and then as she clicked on Katelyn's seat belt, something inside her cracked and she whispered, 'Toby and I slept together when Harper was a baby.'

'You what?' asked Katelyn and Leah shrugged, her heart racing at what was going to happen, but nothing happened.

Instead, Katelyn asked where they were going again.

'I thought you can't remember anything,' says Leah slowly. 'I told you that in the car on the way to the hospital. Have you been lying this whole time?'

'What kind of a friend does such a thing?' asks Katelyn, without answering Leah's question.

'I'm sorry,' says Leah, devastated at how things have turned on her. 'It was once and it was a mistake and... you also...'

'Stop pushing,' shouts Katelyn suddenly, even though Leah is no longer touching her.

Shocked, Leah takes a small step back and then she is in the air, the wind rushing around her, and Katelyn's face, Katelyn's strange smile, is the last thing she sees.

EPILOGUE

Katelyn turns in the large bed and stretches, reaching out to touch Toby who is still asleep.

Outside, the warmth of the Queensland sun is obvious through the small gap in the curtains of the hotel room. It's going to be another beautiful day.

She grabs her phone from the small timber bedside table and quickly checks for messages. Harper is staying with Maureen and Ted for five days while she and Toby have a baby-moon – their last days of freedom before their son arrives.

'You need a break after everything that has happened,' Maureen said a couple of weeks ago, 'and Ted and I need some time with Harper. Just go and have a relaxing time.' Their days away have been perfect with the late spring weather in Queensland, balmy and beautiful.

Scrolling through her phone and reading the news, Katelyn rests her hand on her belly. She is twenty-eight weeks today and her son is an enthusiastic kicker.

It has been a very relaxing holiday and she feels like she and Toby have really reconnected, have really managed to put the last six months behind them.

She and Toby have discussed what happened for hours, trying to figure out how long Leah and Aaron had been planning to break up their marriage. There have been no easy answers.

Leah's terrible death has haunted Katelyn, but each day she manages to let go of everything that happened a little bit more. Leah's shocked expression as her body tipped over the cliff's edge is an image that haunts her nightmares but when she wakes with a racing heart and stares out into the darkness, she reminds herself that it was her or Leah. She did what she had to do.

Everything was made easier by Harper repeating to the police, 'Aunty Leah tried to push Mummy off the cliff.' It was the only thing about that afternoon she remembered properly, that and the chocolate she got when they had returned home. Katelyn had not returned to Teresa's home, but had rung Toby and told him to come and get them. 'Bring a treat for Harper,' she said. 'Bring something big.' She knew that she needed to distract her child.

She and Harper had huddled together at the bottom of the cliff on the street as Katelyn called the police and they waited for Toby to arrive.

'It felt like she was an entirely different person, like she had gone completely crazy,' Katelyn told the detective she spoke to the day after it happened. The detective was an older man, solicitous and kind, letting her go to the bathroom frequently and bringing her juice because he didn't want her to feel unwell. Katelyn kept her hands on her belly most of the time they were talking, protecting her child, protecting her life.

Everyone came to the same conclusion. Katelyn had only been defending herself.

And she had been. It was just luck that Leah went over instead of her. Katelyn shuts her eyes, once again banishing the look on Leah's face as she went over. It could so easily have been her.

She had kept nothing back from the police, telling them about her memory loss and what happened at the party, and explaining about the letter that Leah had torn up and thrown over the cliff. She knew that it was best to tell the truth, the whole truth.

There was no need to lie.

She had only omitted one thing, only chosen to keep one secret, and that was the secret of her exhausted husband telling her he had slept with her best friend when Harper was a baby. Katelyn believes that her memory returned in the middle of a conversation with Toby and perhaps it was what had happened at the party, perhaps it was just that he was so tired of saying the same things, perhaps it was just that he was human and in despair. But she remembers him whispering, 'I slept with Leah, you know. I've done it too. Harper was a baby and you were getting treatment and I had sex with her.'

In the hospital, Katelyn had closed her eyes after he said the words, sinking into shock and sleep. When she opened her eyes again, she had waited for him to repeat himself. And when he hadn't, she had assumed the words were a dream but when she said them to Leah, she understood them to be the truth. Leah's death meant that all of it was behind them now.

Katelyn hadn't gone to the funeral. It would have been inappropriate and she knows she would not have been able to look at the anguish on Teresa and Isaac's faces as they buried their daughter. The detective in charge told Katelyn that Leah's parents had noticed a change in her behaviour in the weeks leading up to Katelyn's party. Her ex-boss at work had talked about how many mistakes she had made, leading to her being fired, and even though he was in trouble with the police himself, Aaron had confirmed that Leah had been strange for weeks.

'I don't know what I would have done if I'd lost you,' Toby keeps saying.

'You didn't,' Katelyn replies. She has assured Toby that she's not going anywhere and that she's never letting anything get in the way of their family again. For one thing, she will never tell Toby that she knows he slept with Leah. He thinks she doesn't remember him telling her and she will keep it that way. It would cause too many problems and lead to many hours of circular discussions which may lead nowhere or may lead to her and Toby separating. She doesn't want that. She could never be a single mother. Instead, she has simply forgiven him and moved on and he seems to have done the same with her. It feels like they have begun again on a level playing field. Maybe she had no idea what she was doing with Aaron the night of her party, or maybe some subconscious part of her knew about Leah and Toby and thought, 'tit for tat'. She never consented. She's sure of that. Even if she wanted it for a moment, she knows she tried to say 'no'. But she can't remember so there will always be a question. She's glad she can't remember.

It's over now. She's let it go.

Everything has felt easier in the last few weeks, like it was meant to be.

'Good morning,' says Toby, his hands sliding over her body. Katelyn smiles, moving closer to him, and she lets herself just enjoy the moment.

Afterwards, as she stands in the shower, she thinks about the nature of truth. She and Toby have told each other everything now and it has brought them closer. Well. Nearly everything.

Katelyn would never have thought herself capable of murder and in her mind she still isn't. It wasn't murder. It was just a push, just a little push. And it wasn't supposed to happen. Katelyn knew what was in the letter. She had read the words already. She just wanted to hear Leah read them aloud and see what she did. Katelyn wasn't stupid and her whole life had been about survival. If anyone was going to survive it was going to be her, but she wanted Leah to know that she knew.

It was going to be the last time they saw each other but Katelyn had no idea it would be something so permanent. No idea at all.

At breakfast Katelyn piles her plate with pancakes and bacon and as she tucks in, Toby says, 'We should have a party when we get back, just something to celebrate that we still have each other, something that lets people see we've moved on with our lives.'

That,' says Katelyn, putting a wedge of pancake into her mouth, 'is an excellent idea.'

A LETTER FROM NICOLE

Hello,

I would like to thank you for taking the time to read *The Day After the Party*.

If you enjoyed this novel and want to keep up to date with all my latest releases, just sign up at the following link. Your email address will never be shared and you can unsubscribe at any time. And you get a free short story as well.

www.bookouture.com/nicole-trope

In this novel Katelyn suffers from transient global amnesia, something I had never heard of until it happened to someone I know. In my research I found out that very little is known about this phenomenon. It was fascinating to research and read about people who have gone through it.

I hope that I have accurately reflected the disorientation and confusion that someone experiencing TGA must feel.

This book is as much about a toxic friendship as it is about TGA. Leah and Katelyn had moments throughout their lives of being terribly jealous of each other and it seemed to me that it was not possible for both of them to survive. Is Katelyn a murderer, or was it self-defence? It's up to you to decide. But whatever you decide, I hope the story has kept you turning the pages on your Kindle, in your book, or kept you listening on audio.

As always, I will be so grateful if you leave a review for the novel.

I love hearing from my readers – you can get in touch through social media. I try to reply to each message I receive.

Thanks again for reading,

Nicole x

facebook.com/NicoleTrope

x.com/nicoletrope

instagram.com/nicoletropeauthor

ACKNOWLEDGEMENTS

I would like to acknowledge and thank my new editor, Ellen Gleeson, for pushing this novel to be the best version it could be. I look forward to many more books with you.

I would especially like to thank Gallit Kessel for sharing her experience of watching a loved one in this situation and for her observations about the episode. It's not easy to discuss this, so thank you for sharing with me.

I would also like to thank Jess Readett for all her work, enthusiasm and patience in answering my emails. She is always a delight to deal with and I could not value that more.

Thanks to Jane Eastgate for the brilliant copy edit and Liz Hatherell for the meticulous proofread.

Thanks to the whole team at Bookouture, including Jenny Geras, Peta Nightingale, Richard King, Alba Proko, Ruth Tross and everyone else involved in producing my audio books and selling rights.

Thanks to my mother, Hilary, who is always ready for a new novel.

Thanks also to David, Mikhayla, Isabella, and Jacob and Jax.

And once again thank you to those who read, review and blog about my work and contact me on Facebook or Twitter to let me know you loved the book. I love hearing your stories and reasons why you have connected with a novel.

Every review is appreciated and I do read them all.

Made in United States
Orlando, FL
23 February 2024

44048115R00146